Travels in the Interior of Africa Volume I

MUNGO PARK

Published in

TABLE OF CONTENTS

INTRODUCTION
VOLUME I. TRAVELS IN THE INTERIOR OF AFRICA
FOOTNOTES

INTRODUCTION

Mungo Park was born on the 10th of September, 1771, the son of a farmer at Fowlshiels, near Selkirk. After studying medicine in Edinburgh, he went out, at the age of twenty-one, assistant-surgeon in a ship bound for the East Indies. When he came back the African Society was in want of an explorer, to take the place of Major Houghton, who had died. Mungo Park volunteered, was accepted, and in his twenty-fourth year, on the 22nd of May, 1795, he sailed for the coasts of Senegal, where he arrived in June.

Thence he proceeded on the travels of which this book is the record. He was absent from England for a little more than two years and a half; returned a few days before Christmas, 1797. He was then twenty-six years old. The African Association published the first edition of his travels as "Travels in the Interior Districts of Africa, 1795-7, by Mungo Park, with an Appendix containing Geographical Illustrations of Africa, by Major Rennell."

Park married, and settled at Peebles in medical practice, but was persuaded by the Government to go out again. He sailed from Portsmouth on the 30th of January, 1805, resolved to trace the Niger to its source or perish in the attempt. He perished. The natives attacked him while passing through a narrow strait of the river at Boussa, and killed him, with all that remained of his party, except one slave. The record of this fatal voyage, partly gathered from his journals, and closed by evidences of the manner of his death, was first published in 1815, as "The Journal of a Mission to the Interior of Africa in 1805, by Mungo Park, together with other Documents, Official and Private, relating to the same Mission. To which is prefixed an Account of the Life of Mr. Park."

MUNGO PARK

H. M.

VOLUME I. TRAVELS IN THE INTERIOR OF AFRICA

CHAPTER I

Soon after my return from the East Indies in 1793, having learned that the noblemen and gentlemen associated for the purpose of prosecuting discoveries in the interior of Africa were desirous of engaging a person to explore that continent, by the way of the Gambia river, I took occasion, through means of the President of the Royal Society, to whom I had the honour to be known, of offering myself for that service.I had been informed that a gentleman of the name of Houghton, a captain in the army, and formerly fort-major at Goree, had already sailed to the Gambia, under the direction of the Association, and that there was reason to apprehend he had fallen a sacrifice to the climate, or perished in some contest with the natives.But this intelligence, instead of deterring me from my purpose, animated me to persist in the offer of my services with the greater solicitude.I had a passionate desire to examine into the productions of a country so little known, and to become experimentally acquainted with the modes of life and character of the natives.I knew that I was able to bear fatigue, and I relied on my youth and the strength of my constitution to preserve me from the effects of the climate.The salary which the committee allowed was sufficiently large, and I made no stipulation for future reward.If I should perish in my journey, I was willing that my hopes and expectations should perish with me; and if I should succeed in rendering the geography of Africa more familiar to my countrymen, and in opening to their ambition and industry new sources of wealth and new channels of commerce, I knew that I was in the hands of men of honour, who would not fail to bestow that remuneration which my successful services should appear to them to merit. The committee of the Association having made such inquiries as they thought necessary, declared themselves satisfied with the qualifications that I possessed, and accepted me for the service; and, with that liberality which on all occasions distinguishes their conduct, gave me every encouragement which it was in their power to grant, or which I could with propriety ask.

It was at first proposed that I should accompany Mr. James Willis, who was then recently appointed consul at Senegambia, and whose countenance in that capacity, it was thought, might have served and protected me; but Government afterwards rescinded his appointment, and I lost that advantage. The kindness of the committee, however, supplied all that was necessary. Being favoured by the secretary of the Association, the late Henry Beaufoy, Esq., with a recommendation to Dr. John Laidley (a gentleman who had resided many years at an English factory on the banks of the Gambia), and furnished with a letter of credit on him for £200, I took my passage in the brig Endeavour - a small vessel trading to the Gambia for beeswax and ivory, commanded by Captain Richard Wyatt - and I became impatient for my departure.

My instructions were very plain and concise. I was directed, on my arrival in Africa, "to pass on to the river Niger, either by way of Bambouk, or by such other route as should be found most convenient. That I should ascertain the course, and, if possible, the rise and termination of that river. That I should use my utmost exertions to visit the principal towns or cities in its neighbourhood, particularly Timbuctoo and Houssa; and that I should be afterwards at liberty to return to Europe, either by the way of the Gambia, or by such other route as, under all the then existing circumstances of my situation and prospects, should appear to me to be most advisable."

We sailed from Portsmouth on the 22nd day of May, 1795. On the 4th of June we saw the mountains over Mogadore, on the coast of Africa; and on the 21st of the same month, after a pleasant voyage of thirty days, we anchored at Jillifrey, a town on the northern bank of the river Gambia, opposite to James's Island, where the English had formerly a small fort.

The kingdom of Barra, in which the town of Jillifrey is situated, produces great plenty of the necessaries of life; but the chief trade of the inhabitants is in salt, which commodity they carry up the river in canoes as high as Barraconda, and bring down in return Indian corn, cotton cloths, elephants' teeth, small quantities of gold dust, andc. The number of canoes and people constantly employed in this trade makes the king of Barra more formidable to Europeans than any other chieftain on the river; and this circumstance probably encouraged him to establish those exorbitant duties which traders of all nations are obliged to pay at entry, amounting to nearly £20 on every vessel, great and small. These duties or customs are generally collected in person by the alkaid, or governor of Jillifrey, and he is attended on these occasions by a numerous train of dependants, among whom are found many who, by their frequent intercourse with the English, have acquired a smattering of our language: but they are commonly very noisy and very troublesome, begging for everything they fancy with such earnestness and importunity, that traders, in order to get quit of them, are frequently obliged to grant their requests.

On the 23rd we departed from Jillifrey, and proceeded to Vintain, a town situated about two miles up a creek on the southern side of the river. This place is much resorted to by Europeans on account of the great quantities of beeswax which are brought hither for sale; the wax is collected in the woods by the Feloops, a wild and unsociable race of people. Their country, which is of considerable extent, abounds in rice; and the natives supply the traders, both on the Gambia and Cassamansa rivers, with that article, and also with goats and poultry, on very reasonable terms. The honey which they collect is chiefly used by themselves in making a strong intoxicating liquor, much the same as the mead which is produced from honey in Great Britain. In their traffic with Europeans, the Feloops generally employ a factor or agent of the Mandingo nation, who speaks a little English, and is acquainted with the trade of the river. This broker makes the bargain; and, with the connivance of the European, receives a certain part only of the payment, which he gives to his employer as the whole; the remainder (which is very truly called the cheating money) he receives when the Feloop is gone, and appropriates to himself as a reward for his trouble.

The language of the Feloops is appropriate and peculiar; and as their trade is chiefly conducted, as hath been observed, by Mandingoes, the Europeans have no inducement to learn it.

On the 26th we left Vintain, and continued our course up the river, anchoring whenever the tide failed us, and frequently towing the vessel with the boat. The river is deep and muddy; the banks are covered with impenetrable thickets of mangrove; and the whole of the adjacent country appears to be flat and swampy.

The Gambia abounds with fish, some species of which are excellent food; but none of them that I recollect are known in Europe. At the entrance from the sea sharks are found in great abundance, and, higher up, alligators and the hippopotamus (or river-horse) are very numerous.

In six days after leaving Vintain we reached Jonkakonda, a place of considerable trade, where our vessel was to take in part of her lading. The next morning the several European traders came from their different factories to receive their letters, and learn the nature and amount of her cargo; and the captain despatched a messenger to Dr. Laidley to inform him of my arrival. He came to Jonkakonda the morning following, when I delivered him Mr. Beaufoy's letter, and he gave me a kind invitation to spend my time at his house until an opportunity should offer of prosecuting my journey. This invitation was too acceptable to be refused, and being furnished by the Doctor with a horse and guide, I set out from Jonkakonda at daybreak on the 5th of July, and at eleven o'clock arrived at Pisania, where I was accommodated with a room and other conveniences in the Doctor's house.

Pisania is a small village in the king of Yany's dominions, established by British subjects as a factory for trade, and inhabited solely by them and their black servants. It is situated on the banks of the Gambia, sixteen miles above Jonkakonda. The white residents, at the time of may arrival there, consisted only of Dr. Laidley, and two gentlemen who were brothers, of the name of Ainsley; but their domestics were numerous. They enjoyed perfect security under the king's protection, and being highly esteemed and respected by the natives at large, wanted no accommodation or comfort which the country could supply, and the greatest part of the trade in slaves, ivory, and gold was in their hands.

Being now settled for some time at my ease, my first object was to learn the Mandingo tongue, being the language in almost general use throughout this part of Africa, and without which I was fully convinced that I never could acquire an extensive knowledge of the country or its inhabitants. In this pursuit I was greatly assisted by Dr. Laidley.

In researches of this kind, and in observing the manners and customs of the natives, in a country so little known to the nations of Europe, and furnished with so many striking and uncommon objects of nature, my time passed not unpleasantly, and I began to flatter myself that I had escaped the fever, or seasoning, to which Europeans, on their first arrival in hot climates, are generally subject. But on the 31st of July I imprudently exposed myself to the night-dew in observing an eclipse of the moon, with a view to determine the longitude of the place; the next day I found myself attacked with a smart fever and delirium, and such an illness followed as confined me to the house during the greatest part of August. My recovery was very slow, but I embraced every short interval of convalescence to walk out, and make myself acquainted with the productions of the country.

In one of those excursions, having rambled farther than usual, on a hot day, I brought on a return of my fever, and on the 10th of September I was again confined to my bed. The fever, however, was not so violent as before; and in the course of three weeks I was able, when the weather would permit, to renew my botanical excursions; and when it rained, I amused myself with drawing plants, andc., in my chamber. The care and attention of Dr. Laidley contributed greatly to alleviate my sufferings; his company and conversation beguiled the tedious hours during that gloomy season, when the rain falls in torrents; when suffocating heats oppress by day, and when the night is spent by the terrified travellers in listening to the croaking of frogs (of which the numbers are beyond imagination), the shrill cry of the jackal, and the deep howling of the hyæna, a dismal concert, interrupted only by the roar of such tremendous thunder as no person can form a conception of but those who have heard it.

The country itself being an immense level, and very generally covered with wood, presents a tiresome and gloomy uniformity to the eye; but although Nature has denied to the inhabitants the beauties of romantic landscapes, she has bestowed on them, with a liberal hand, the more important blessings of fertility and abundance. A little attention to cultivation procures a sufficiency of corn, the fields afford a rich pasturage for cattle, and the natives are plentifully supplied with excellent fish, both from the Gambia river and the Walli creek.

The grains which are chiefly cultivated are - Indian corn (zea mays); two kinds of holcus spicatus, called by the natives soono and sanio; holcus niger, and holcus bicolor, the former of which they have named bassi woolima, and the latter bassiqui. These, together with rice, are raised in considerable quantities; besides which, the inhabitants in the vicinity of the towns and villages have gardens which produce onions, calavances, yams, cassavi, ground nuts, pompions, gourds, water-melons, and some other esculent plants.

I observed likewise, near the towns, small patches of cotton and indigo. The former of these articles supplies them with clothing, and with the latter they dye their cloth of an excellent blue colour, in a manner that will hereafter be described.

In preparing their corn for food, the natives use a large wooden mortar called a paloon, in which they bruise the seed until it parts with the outer covering, or husk, which is then separated from the clean corn by exposing it to the wind, nearly in the same manner as wheat is cleared from the chaff in England. The corn thus freed from the husk is returned to the mortar and beaten into meal, which is dressed variously in different countries; but the most common preparation of it among the nations of the Gambia is a sort of pudding which they call kouskous. It is made by first moistening the flour with water, and then stirring and shaking it about in a large calabash, or gourd, till it adheres together in small granules resembling sago. It is then put into an earthen pot, whose bottom is perforated with a number of small holes; and this pot being placed upon another, the two vessels are luted together either with a paste of meal and water, or with cows' dung, and placed upon the fire. In the lower vessel is commonly some animal food and water, the steam or vapour of which ascends through the perforations in the bottom of the upper vessel, and softens and the kouskous, which is very much esteemed throughout all the countries that I visited. I am informed that the same manner of preparing flour is very generally used on the Barbary coast, and that the dish so prepared is there called by the same name. It is therefore probable that the negroes borrowed the practice from the Moors.

Their domestic animals are nearly the same as in Europe. Swine are found in the woods, but their flesh is not esteemed. Probably the marked abhorrence in which this animal is held by the votaries of Mohammed has spread itself among the pagans. Poultry of all kinds, the turkey excepted, is everywhere to be had. The guinea-fowl and red partridge abound in the fields, and the woods furnish a small species of antelope, of which the venison is highly and deservedly prized.

Of the other wild animals in the Mandingo countries, the most common are the hyæna, the panther, and the elephant. Considering the use that is made of the latter in the East Indies, it may be thought extraordinary that the natives of Africa have not, in any part of this immense continent, acquired the skill of taming this powerful and docile creature, and applying his strength and faculties to the service of man. When I told some of the natives that this was actually done in the countries of the East, my auditors laughed me to scorn, and exclaimed, "Tobaubo fonnio!" ("A white man's lie!") The negroes frequently find means to destroy the elephant by firearms; they hunt it principally for the sake of the teeth, which they transfer in barter to those who sell them again to the Europeans. The flesh they eat, and consider it as a great delicacy.

On the 6th of October the waters of the Gambia were at the greatest height, being fifteen feet above the high-water mark of the tide, after which they began to subside, at first slowly, but afterwards very rapidly, sometimes sinking more than a foot in twenty-four hours. By the beginning of November the river had sunk to its former level, and the tide ebbed and flowed as usual. When the river had subsided, and the atmosphere grew dry, I recovered apace, and began to think of my departure, for this is reckoned the most proper season for travelling. The natives had completed their harvest, and provisions were everywhere cheap and plentiful.

Dr. Laidley was at this time employed in a trading voyage at Jonkakonda. I wrote to him to desire that he would use his interest with the slatees, or slave-merchants, to procure me the company and protection of the first coffle (or caravan) that might leave Gambia for the interior country; and, in the meantime, I requested him to purchase for me a horse and two asses. A few days afterwards the Doctor returned to Pisania, and informed me that a coffle would certainly go for the interior in the course of the dry season; but that, as many of the merchants belonging to it had not yet completed their assortment of goods, he could not say at what time they would set out.

As the characters and dispositions of the slatees, and people that composed the caravan, were entirely unknown to me - and as they seemed rather averse to my purpose, and unwilling to enter into any positive engagements on my account - and the time of their departure being withal very uncertain, I resolved, on further deliberation, to avail myself of the dry season, and proceed without them.

Dr. Laidley approved my determination, and promised me every assistance in his power to enable me to prosecute my journey with comfort and safety. This resolution having been formed, I made preparations accordingly.

And now, being about to take leave of my hospitable friend (whose kindness and solicitude continued to the moment of my departure), and to quit for many months the countries bordering on the Gambia, it seems proper, before I proceed with my narrative, that I should in this place give some account of the several negro nations which inhabit the banks of this celebrated river, and the commercial intercourse that subsists between them, and such of the nations of Europe as find their advantage in trading to this part of Africa. The observations which have occurred to me on both these subjects will be found in the following chapter.

CHAPTER II

The natives of the countries bordering on the Gambia, though distributed into a great many distinct governments, may, I think, be divided into four great classes - the Feloops, the Jaloffs, the Foulahs, and the Mandingoes. Among all these nations, the religion of Mohammed has made, and continues to make, considerable progress; but in most of them the body of the people, both free and enslaved, persevere in maintaining the blind but harmless superstitions of their ancestors, and are called by the Mohammedans kafirs, or infidels.

Of the Feloops, I have little to add to what has been observed concerning them in the former chapter. They are of a gloomy disposition, and are supposed never to forgive an injury. They are even said to transmit their quarrels as deadly feuds to their posterity, insomuch that a son considers it as incumbent on him, from a just sense of filial obligation, to become the avenger of his deceased father's wrongs. If a man loses his life in one of these sudden quarrels which perpetually occur at their feasts, when the whole party is intoxicated with mead, his son, or the eldest of his sons (if he has more than one), endeavours to procure his father's sandals, which he wears once a year, on the anniversary of his father's death, until a fit opportunity offers of revenging his fate, when the object of his resentment seldom escapes his pursuit. This fierce and unrelenting disposition is, however, counterbalanced by many good qualities: they display the utmost gratitude and affection towards their benefactors, and the fidelity with which they preserve whatever is entrusted to them is remarkable. During the present war, they have more than once taken up arms to defend our merchant vessels from French privateers; and English property of considerable value has frequently been left at Vintain for a long time entirely under the care of the Feloops, who have uniformly manifested on such occasions the strictest honesty and punctuality. How greatly is it to be wished that the minds of a people so determined and faithful could be softened and civilised by the mild and benevolent spirit of Christianity!

The Jaloffs (or Yaloffs) are an active, powerful, and warlike race, inhabiting great part of that tract which lies between the river Senegal and the Mandingo states on the Gambia; yet they differ from the Mandingoes not only in language, but likewise in complexion and features. The noses of the Jaloffs are not so much depressed, nor the lips so protuberant, as among the generality of Africans; and although their skin is of the deepest black, they are considered by the white traders as the most sightly negroes on this part of the continent.

Their language is said to be copious and significant, and is often learnt by Europeans trading to Senegal.

The Foulahs (or Pholeys), such of them at least as reside near the Gambia, are chiefly of a tawny complexion, with soft silky hair, and pleasing features. They are much attached to a pastoral life, and have introduced themselves into all the kingdoms on the windward coast as herdsmen and husbandmen, paying a tribute to the sovereign of the country for the lands which they hold. Not having many opportunities, however, during my residence at Pisania, of improving my acquaintance with these people, I defer entering at large into their character until a fitter occasion occurs, which will present itself when I come to Bondou.

The Mandingoes, of whom it remains to speak, constitute, in truth, the bulk of the inhabitants in all those districts of Africa which I visited; and their language, with a few exceptions, is universally understood and very generally spoken in that part of the continent.

They are called Mandingoes, I conceive, as having originally migrated from the interior state of Manding, of which some account will hereafter be given.

In every considerable town there is a chief magistrate, called the alkaid, whose office is hereditary, and whose business it is to preserve order, to levy duties on travellers, and to preside at all conferences in the exercise of local jurisdiction and the administration of justice. These courts are composed of the elders of the town (of free condition), and are termed palavers; and their proceedings are conducted in the open air with sufficient solemnity. Both sides of a question are freely canvassed, witnesses are publicly examined, and the decisions which follow generally meet with the approbation of the surrounding audience.

As the negroes have no written language of their own, the general rule of decision is an appeal to ancient custom; but since the system of Mohammed has made so great progress among them, the converts to that faith have gradually introduced, with the religious tenets, many of the civil institutions of the prophet; and where the Koran is not found sufficiently explicit, recourse is had to a commentary called Al Sharra, containing, as I was told, a complete exposition or digest of the Mohammedan laws, both civil and criminal, properly arranged and illustrated.

This frequency of appeal to written laws, with which the pagan natives are necessarily unacquainted, has given rise in their palavers to (what I little expected to find in Africa) professional advocates, or expounders of the law, who are allowed to appear and to plead for plaintiff or defendant, much in the same manner as counsel in the law-courts of Great Britain. They are Mohammedan negroes, who have made, or affect to have made, the laws of the prophet their peculiar study; and if I may judge from their harangues, which I frequently attended, I believe, that in the forensic qualifications of procrastination and cavil, and the arts of confounding and perplexing a cause, they are not always surpassed by the ablest pleaders in Europe. While I was at Pisania, a cause was heard which furnished the Mohammedan lawyers with an admirable opportunity of displaying their professional dexterity. The case was this:- An ass belonging to a Serawoolli negro (a native of an interior country near the river Senegal) had broke into a field of corn belonging to one of the Mandingo inhabitants, and destroyed great part of it. The Mandingo having caught the animal in his field, immediately drew his knife and cut his throat. The Serawoolli thereupon called a palaver (or in European terms, brought an action) to recover damages for the loss of his beast, on which he set a high value. The defendant confessed he had killed the ass, but pleaded a set-off, insisting that the loss he had sustained by the ravage in his corn was equal to the sum demanded for the animal. To ascertain this fact was the point at issue, and the learned advocates contrived to puzzle the cause in such a manner that, after a hearing of three days, the court broke up without coming to any determination upon it; and a second palaver was, I suppose, thought necessary.

The Mandingoes, generally speaking, are of a mild, sociable, and obliging disposition. The men are commonly above the middle size, well-shaped, strong, and capable of enduring great labour. The women are good-natured, sprightly, and agreeable. The dress of both sexes is composed of cotton cloth of their own manufacture: that of the men is a loose frock, not unlike a surplice, with drawers which reach half-way down the leg; and they wear sandals on their feet, and white cotton caps on their heads. The women's dress consists of two pieces of cloth, each of which is about six feet long and three broad. One of these they wrap round their waist, which, hanging down to the ankles, answers the purpose of a petticoat; the other is thrown negligently over the bosom and shoulders.

This account of their clothing is indeed nearly applicable to the natives of all the different countries in this part of Africa; a peculiar national mode is observable only in the head-dresses of the women.

Thus, in the countries of the Gambia, the females wear a sort of bandage, which they call jalla.It is a narrow strip of cotton cloth wrapped many times round, immediately over the forehead.In Bondou, the head is encircled with strings of white beads, and a small plate of gold is worn in the middle of the forehead.In Kasson the ladies decorate their heads in a very tasteful and elegant manner with white seashells.In Kaarta and Ludamar, the women raise their hair to a great height by the addition of a pad (as the ladies did formerly in Great Britain), which they decorate with a species of coral brought from the Red Sea by pilgrims returning from Mecca, and sold at a great price.

In the construction of their dwelling-houses the Mandingoes also conform to the general practice of the African nations in this part of the continent, contenting themselves with small and incommodious hovels.A circular mud wall, about four feet high, upon which is placed a conical roof, composed of the bamboo cane, and thatched with grass, forms alike the palace of the king and the hovel of the slave.Their household furniture is equally simple.A hurdle of canes placed upon upright sticks, about two feet from the ground, upon which is spread a mat or bullock's hide, answers the purpose of a bed; a water jar, some earthen pots for dressing their food; a few wooden bowls and calabashes, and one or two low stools, compose the rest.

As every man of free condition has a plurality of wives, it is found necessary (to prevent, I suppose, matrimonial disputes) that each of the ladies should be accommodated with a hut to herself; and all the huts belonging to the same family are surrounded by a fence constructed of bamboo canes, split and formed into a sort of wicker-work.The whole enclosure is called a sirk, or surk.A number of these enclosures, with narrow passages between them, form what is called a town; but the huts are generally placed without any regularity, according to the caprice of the owner.The only rule that seems to be attended to is placing the door towards the south-west, in order to admit the sea-breeze.

In each town is a large stage called the bentang, which answers the purpose of a public hall or town house.It is composed of interwoven canes, and is generally sheltered from the sun by being erected in the shade of some large tree.It is here that all public affairs are transacted and trials conducted; and here the lazy and indolent meet to smoke their pipes, and hear the news of the day.In most of the towns the Mohammedans have also a missura, or mosque, in which they assemble and offer up their daily prayers, according to the rules of the Koran.

In the account which I have thus given of the natives, the reader must bear in mind that my observations apply chiefly to persons of free condition, who constitute, I suppose, not more than one-fourth part of the inhabitants at large.The other three-fourths are in a state of hopeless and hereditary slavery, and are employed in cultivating the land, in the care of cattle, and in servile offices of all kinds, much in the same manner as the slaves in the West Indies.I was told, however, that the Mandingo master can neither deprive his slave of life, nor sell him to a stranger, without first calling a palaver on his conduct, or in other words, bringing him to a public trial.But this degree of protection is extended only to the native or domestic slave.Captives taken in war, and those unfortunate victims who are condemned to slavery for crimes or insolvency - and, in short, all those unhappy people who are brought down from the interior countries for sale - have no security whatever, but may be treated and disposed of in all respects as the owner thinks proper.It sometimes happens, indeed, when no ships are on the coast, that a humane and considerate master incorporates his purchased slaves among his domestics; and their offspring at least, if not the parents, become entitled to all the privileges of the native class.

The earliest European establishment on this celebrated river was a factory of the Portuguese, and to this must be ascribed the introduction of the numerous words of that language which are still in use among the negroes.The Dutch, French, and English afterwards successively possessed themselves of settlements on the coast; but the trade of the Gambia became, and continued for many years, a sort of monopoly in the hands of the English.In the travels of Francis Moore is preserved an account of the Royal African Company's establishments in this river in the year 1730; at which the James's factory alone consisted of a governor, deputy-governor, and two other principal officers; eight factors, thirteen writers, twenty inferior attendants and tradesmen; a company of soldiers, and thirty-two negro servants; besides sloops, shallops, and boats, with their crews; and there were no less than eight subordinate factories in other parts of the river.

The trade with Europe, by being afterwards laid open, was almost annihilated.The share which the subjects of England at this time hold in it supports not more than two or three annual ships; and I am informed that the gross value of British exports is under £20,000.The French and Danes still maintain a small share, and the Americans have lately sent a few vessels to the Gambia by way of experiment.

The commodities exported to the Gambia from Europe consist chiefly of firearms and ammunition, iron-ware, spirituous liquors, tobacco, cotton caps, a small quantity of broadcloth, and a few articles of the manufacture of Manchester; a small assortment of India goods, with some glass beads, amber, and other trifles, for which are taken in exchange slaves, gold dust, ivory, beeswax, and hides.Slaves are the chief article, but the whole number which at this time are annually exported from the Gambia by all nations is supposed to be under one thousand.

Most of these unfortunate victims are brought to the coast in periodical caravans; many of them from very remote inland countries, for the language which they speak is not understood by the inhabitants of the maritime districts.In a subsequent part of my work I shall give the best information I have been able to collect concerning the manner in which they are obtained.On their arrival at the coast, if no immediate opportunity offers of selling them to advantage, they are distributed among the neighbouring villages, until a slave ship arrives, or until they can be sold to black traders, who sometimes purchase on speculation.In the meanwhile, the poor wretches are kept constantly fettered, two and two of them being chained together, and employed in the labours of the field, and, I am sorry to add, are very scantily fed, as well as harshly treated.The price of a slave varies according to the number of purchasers from Europe, and the arrival of caravans from the interior; but in general I reckon that a young and healthy male, from sixteen to twenty-five years of age, may be estimated on the spot from £18 to £20 sterling.

The negro slave-merchants, as I have observed in the former chapter, are called slatees, who, besides slaves, and the merchandise which they bring for sale to the whites, supply the inhabitants of the maritime districts with native iron, sweet-smelling gums and frankincense, and a commodity called shea-toulou, which, literally translated, signifies tree-butter.

In payment of these articles, the maritime states supply the interior countries with salt, a scarce and valuable commodity, as I frequently and painfully experienced in the course of my journey.Considerable quantities of this article, however, are also supplied to the inland natives by the Moors, who obtain it from the salt pits in the Great Desert, and receive in return corn, cotton cloth, and slaves.

In their early intercourse with Europeans the article that attracted most notice was iron.Its utility, in forming the instruments of war and husbandry, make it preferable to all others, and iron soon became the measure by which the value of all other commodities was ascertained.Thus, a certain quantity of goods, of whatever denomination, appearing to be equal in value to a bar of iron, constituted, in the traders' phraseology, a bar of that particular merchandise.Twenty leaves of tobacco, for instance, were considered as a bar of tobacco; and a gallon of spirits (or rather half spirits and half water) as a bar of rum, a bar of one commodity being reckoned equal in value to a bar of another commodity.

As, however, it must unavoidably happen that, according to the plenty or scarcity of goods at market in proportion to the demand, the relative value would be subject to continual fluctuation, greater precision has been found necessary; and at this time the current value of a single bar of any kind is fixed by the whites at two shillings sterling.Thus, a slave whose price is £15, is said to be worth 150 bars.

In transactions of this nature it is obvious that the white trader has infinitely the advantage over the African, whom, therefore, it is difficult to satisfy, for conscious of his own ignorance, he naturally becomes exceedingly suspicious and wavering; and, indeed, so very unsettled and jealous are the negroes in their dealings with the whites, that a bargain is never considered by the European as concluded until the purchase money is paid and the party has taken leave.

Having now brought together such general observations on the country and its inhabitants as occurred to me during my residence in the vicinity of the Gambia, I shall detain the reader no longer with introductory matter, but proceed, in the next chapter, to a regular detail of the incidents which happened, and the reflections which arose in my mind, in the course of my painful and perilous journey, from its commencement until my return to the Gambia.

CHAPTER III

On the 2nd of December, 1795, I took my departure from the hospitable mansion of Dr. Laidley.I was fortunately provided with a negro servant who spoke both the English and Mandingo tongues.His name was Johnson.He was a native of this part of Africa, and having in his youth been conveyed to Jamaica as a slave, he had been made free, and taken to England by his master, where he had resided many years, and at length found his way back to his native country.As he was known to Dr. Laidley, the Doctor recommended him to me, and I hired him as my interpreter, at the rate of ten bars monthly to be paid to himself, and five bars a month to be paid to his wife during his absence.Dr. Laidley furthermore provided me with a negro boy of his own, named Demba, a sprightly youth, who, besides Mandingo, spoke the language of the Serawoollies, an inland people (of whom mention will hereafter be made) residing on the banks of the Senegal; and to induce him to behave well, the Doctor promised him his freedom on his return, in case I should report favourably of his fidelity and services.I was furnished with a horse for myself (a small but very hardy and spirited beast, which cost me to the value of £7 10s), and two asses for my interpreter and servant.My baggage was light, consisting chiefly of provisions for two days; a small assortment of beads, amber, and tobacco, for the purchase of a fresh supply as I proceeded; a few changes of linen, and other necessary apparel; an umbrella, a pocket sextant, a magnetic compass, and a thermometer; together with two fowling-pieces, two pair of pistols, and some other small articles.

A free man (a bashreen, or Mohammedan) named Madiboo, who was travelling to the kingdom of Bambara, and two slatees, or slave merchants, of the Serawoolli nation, and of the same sect, who were going to Bondou, offered their services, as far as they intended respectively to proceed, as did likewise a negro named Tami (also a Mohammedan), a native of Kasson, who had been employed some years by Dr. Laidley as a blacksmith, and was returning to his native country with the savings of his labours. All these men travelled on foot, driving their asses before them.

Thus I had no less than six attendants, all of whom had been taught to regard me with great respect, and to consider that their safe return hereafter to the countries on the Gambia would depend on my preservation.

Dr. Laidley himself, and Messrs. Ainsley, with a number of their domestics, kindly determined to accompany me the first two days; and I believe they secretly thought they should never see me afterwards.

We reached Jindey the same day, having crossed the Walli creek, a branch of the Gambia, and rested at the house of a black woman, who had formerly been the paramour of a white trader named Hewett, and who, in consequence thereof, was called, by way of distinction, seniora. In the evening we walked out to see an adjoining village, belonging to a slatee named Jemaffoo Momadoo, the richest of all the Gambia traders. We found him at home, and he thought so highly of the honour done him by this visit, that he presented us with a fine bullock, which was immediately killed, and part of it dressed for our evening's repast.

The negroes do not go to supper till late, and, in order to amuse ourselves while our beef was preparing, a Mandingo was desired to relate some diverting stories, in listening to which, and smoking tobacco, we spent three hours. These stories bear some resemblance to those in the Arabian Nights' Entertainments, but, in general, are of a more ludicrous cast.

About one o'clock in the afternoon of the 3rd of December, I took my leave of Dr. Laidley and Messrs. Ainsley, and rode slowly into the woods. I had now before me a boundless forest, and a country, the inhabitants of which were strangers to civilised life, and to most of whom a white man was the object of curiosity or plunder. I reflected that I had parted from the last European I might probably behold, and perhaps quitted for ever the comforts of Christian society. Thoughts like these would necessarily cast a gloom over my mind; and I rode musing along for about three miles, when I was awakened from my reverie by a body of people, who came running up, and stopped the asses, giving me to understand that I must go with them to Peckaba, to present myself to the king of Walli, or pay customs to them. I endeavoured to make them comprehend that the object of my journey not being traffic, I ought not to be subjected to a tax like the slatees, and other merchants, who travel for gain; but I reasoned to no purpose. They said it was usual for travellers of all descriptions to make a present to the king of Walli, and without doing so I could not be permitted to proceed. As they were more numerous than my attendants, and withal very noisy, I thought it prudent to comply with their demand; and having presented them with four bars of tobacco, for the king's use, I was permitted to continue my journey, and at sunset reached a village near

Kootacunda, where we rested for the night.

In the morning of December 4th I passed Kootacunda, the last town of Walli, and stopped about an hour at a small adjoining village to pay customs to an officer of the king of Woolli; we rested the ensuing night at a village called Tabajang; and at noon the next day (December 5th) we reached Medina, the capital of the king of Woolli's dominions.

The kingdom of Woolli is bounded by Walli on the west, by the Gambia on the south, by the small river Walli on the north-west, by Bondou on the north-east, and on the east by the Simbani wilderness.

The inhabitants are Mandingoes, and, like most of the Mandingo nations, are divided into two great sects - the Mohammedans, who are called bushreens, and the pagans, who are called indiscriminately kafirs (unbelievers) and sonakies (i.e., men who drink strong liquors). The pagan natives are by far the most numerous, and the government of the country is in their hands; for though the most respectable among the bushreens are frequently consulted in affairs of importance, yet they are never permitted to take any share in the executive government, which rests solely in the hands of the mansa, or sovereign, and great officers of the state. Of these, the first in point of rank is the presumptive heir of the crown, who is called the farbanna. Next to him are the alkaids, or provincial governors, who are more frequently called keamos. Then follow the two grand divisions of freemen and slaves; of the former, the slatees, so frequently mentioned in the preceding pages, are considered as the principal; but, in all classes, great respect is paid to the authority of aged men.

On the death of the reigning monarch, his eldest son (if he has attained the age of manhood) succeeds to the regal authority. If there is no son, or if the son is under the age of discretion, a meeting of the great men is held, and the late monarch's nearest relation (commonly his brother) is called to the government, not as regent, or guardian to the infant son, but in full right, and to the exclusion of the minor. The charges of the government are defrayed by occasional tributes from the people, and by duties on goods transported across the country. Travellers, on going from the Gambia towards the interior, pay customs in European merchandise. On returning, they pay in iron and shea-toulou. These taxes are paid at every town.

Medina, the capital of the kingdom, at which I was now arrived, is a place of considerable extent, and may contain from eight hundred to one thousand houses. It is fortified in the common African manner, by a surrounding high wall built of clay, and an outward fence of pointed stakes and prickly bushes; but the walls are neglected, and the outward fence has suffered considerably from the active hands of busy housewives, who pluck up the stakes for firewood. I obtained a lodging at one of the king's near relations, who apprised me that at my introduction to the king I must not presume to shake hands with him. "It was not usual," he said, "to allow this liberty to strangers."Thus instructed, I went in the afternoon to pay my respects to the sovereign, and ask permission to pass through his territories to Bondou.The king's name was Jatta.He was the same venerable old man of whom so favourable an account was transmitted by Major Houghton.I found him seated upon a mat before the door of his hut; a number of men and women were arranged on each side, who were singing and clapping their hands.I saluted him respectfully, and informed him of the purport of my visit.The king graciously replied, that he not only gave me leave to pass through his country, but would offer up his prayers for my safety.On this, one of my attendants, seemingly in return for the king's condescension, began to sing, or rather to roar an Arabic song, at every pause of which the king himself, and all the people present, struck their hands against their foreheads, and exclaimed, with devout and affecting solemnity, "Amen, amen!"The king told me, furthermore, that I should have a guide the day following, who would conduct me safely to the frontier of his kingdom - I then took my leave, and in the evening sent the king an order upon Dr. Laidley for three gallons of rum, and received in return great store of provisions.

December 6. - Early in the morning I went to the king a second time, to learn if the guide was ready.I found his Majesty seated upon a bullock's hide, warming himself before a large fire, for the Africans are sensible of the smallest variation in the temperature of the air, and frequently complain of cold when a European is oppressed with heat.He received me with a benevolent countenance, and tenderly entreated me to desist from my purpose of travelling into the interior, telling me that Major Houghton had been killed in his route, and that if I followed his footsteps I should probably meet with his fate.He said that I must not judge of the people of the eastern country by those of Woolli: that the latter were acquainted with white men, and respected them, whereas the people of the east had never seen a white man, and would certainly destroy me.I thanked the king for his affectionate solicitude, but told him that I had considered the matter, and was determined, notwithstanding all dangers, to proceed.The king shook his head, but desisted from further persuasion, and told me the guide should be ready in the afternoon.

About two o'clock, the guide appearing, I went and took my last farewell of the good old king, and in three hours reached Konjour, a small village, where we determined to rest for the night.Here I purchased a fine sheep for some beads, and my Serawoolli attendants killed it with all the ceremonies prescribed by their religion.Part of it was dressed for supper, after which a dispute arose between one of the Serawoolli negroes, and Johnson, my interpreter, about the sheep's horns.The former claimed the horns as his perquisite, for having acted the part of our butcher, and Johnson contested the claim.I settled the matter by giving a horn to each of them.This trifling incident is mentioned as introductory to what follows, for it appeared on inquiry that these horns were highly valued, as being easily convertible into portable sheaths, or cases, for containing and keeping secure certain charms or amulets called saphies, which the negroes constantly wear about them.These saphies are prayers, or rather sentences, from the Koran, which the Mohammedan priests write on scraps of paper, and sell to the simple natives, who consider them to possess very extraordinary virtues.Some of the negroes wear them to guard themselves against the bite of snakes or alligators; and on this occasion the saphie is commonly enclosed in a snake's or alligator's skin, and tied round the ankle.Others have recourse to them in time of war, to protect their persons against hostile weapons; but the common use to which these amulets are applied is to prevent or cure bodily diseases - to preserve from hunger and thirst - and generally to conciliate the favour of superior powers, under all the circumstances and occurrences of life. {1}

In this case it is impossible not to admire the wonderful contagion of superstition, for, notwithstanding that the majority of the negroes are pagans, and absolutely reject the doctrines of Mohammed, I did not meet with a man, whether a bushreen or kafir, who was not fully persuaded of the powerful efficacy of these amulets.The truth is, that all the natives of this part of Africa consider the art of writing as bordering on magic; and it is not in the doctrines of the prophet, but in the arts of the magician, that their confidence is placed.It will hereafter be seen that I was myself lucky enough, in circumstances of distress, to turn the popular credulity in this respect to good account.

On the 7th I departed from Konjour, and slept at a village called Malla (or Mallaing), and on the 8th about noon I arrived at Kolor, a considerable town, near the entrance into which I observed, hanging upon a tree, a sort of masquerade habit, made of the bark of trees, which I was told, on inquiry, belonged to Mumbo Jumbo.This is a strange bugbear, common to all the Mandingo towns, and much employed by the pagan natives in keeping their women in subjection; for as the kafirs are not restricted in the number of their wives, every one marries as many as he can conveniently maintain - and as it frequently happens that the ladies disagree among themselves, family quarrels sometimes rise to such a height, that the authority of the husband can no longer preserve peace in his household.In such cases, the interposition of Mumbo Jumbo is called in, and is always decisive.

This strange minister of justice (who is supposed to be either the husband himself, or some person instructed by him), disguised in the dress that has been mentioned, and armed with the rod of public authority, announces his coming (whenever his services are required) by loud and dismal screams in the woods near the town.He begins the pantomime at the approach of night; and as soon as it is dark he enters the town, and proceeds to the bentang, at which all the inhabitants immediately assemble.

December 9. - As there was no water to be procured on the road, we travelled with great expedition until we reached Tambacunda; and departing from thence early the next morning, the 10th, we reached in the evening Kooniakary, a town of nearly the same magnitude as Kolor. About noon on the 11th we arrived at Koojar, the frontier town of Woolli, towards Bondou, from which it is separated by an intervening wilderness of two days' journey.

The guide appointed by the king of Woolli being now to return, I presented him with some amber for his trouble; and having been informed that it was not possible at all times to procure water in the wilderness, I made inquiry for men who would serve both as guides and water-bearers during my journey across it. Three negroes, elephant-hunters, offered their services for these purposes, which I accepted, and paid them three bars each in advance; and the day being far spent, I determined to pass the night in my present quarters.

The inhabitants of Koojar, though not wholly unaccustomed to the sight of Europeans (most of them having occasionally visited the countries on the Gambia), beheld me with a mixture of curiosity and reverence, and in the evening invited me to see a neobering, or wrestling-match, at the bentang. This is an exhibition very common in all the Mandingo countries. The spectators arranged themselves in a circle, leaving the intermediate space for the wrestlers, who were strong active young men, full of emulation, and accustomed, I suppose, from their infancy to this sort of exertion. Being stripped of their clothing, except a short pair of drawers, and having their skin anointed with oil, or shea butter, the combatants approached each other on all-fours, parrying with, and occasionally extending a hand for some time, till at length one of them sprang forward, and caught his rival by the knee. Great dexterity and judgment were now displayed, but the contest was decided by superior strength; and I think that few Europeans would have been able to cope with the conqueror. It must not be unobserved, that the combatants were animated by the music of a drum, by which their actions were in some measure regulated.

The wrestling was succeeded by a dance, in which many performers assisted, all of whom were provided with little bells, which were fastened to their legs and arms; and here, too, the drum regulated their motions. It was beaten with a crooked stick, which the drummer held in his right hand, occasionally using his left to deaden the sound, and thus vary the music. The drama is likewise applied on these occasions to keep order among the spectators, by imitating the sound of certain Mandingo sentences. For example, when the wrestling-match is about to begin, the drummer strikes what is understood to signify ali bæ see (sit all down), upon which the spectators immediately seat themselves; and when the combatants are to begin, he strikes amuta! amuta! (take hold! take hold!)

In the course of the evening I was presented, by way of refreshment, with a liquor, which tasted so much like the strong beer of my native country (and very good beer too), as to induce me to inquire into its composition; and I learnt, with some degree of surprise, that it was actually made from corn which had been previously malted, much in the same manner as barley is malted in Great Britain. A root yielding a grateful bitter was used in lieu of hops, the name of which I have forgotten; but the corn which yields the wort is the holcus spicatus of botanists.

Early in the morning (the 12th) I found that one of the elephant-hunters had absconded with the money he had received from me in part of wages; and in order to prevent the other two from following his example, I made them instantly fill their calabashes (or gourds) with water; and as the sun rose, I entered the wilderness that separates the kingdoms of Woolli and Bondou.

We continued our journey without stopping any more until noon, when we came to a large tree, called by the natives neema taba. It had a very singular appearance, being decorated with innumerable rags or scraps of cloth, which persons travelling across the wilderness had at different times tied to the branches, probably at first to inform the traveller that water was to be found near it; but the custom has been so greatly sanctioned by time, that nobody now presumes to pass without hanging up something. I followed the example, and suspended a handsome piece of cloth on one of the boughs; and being told that either a well, or pool of water, was at no great distance, I ordered the negroes to unload the asses, that we might give them corn, and regale ourselves with the provisions we had brought. In the meantime, I sent one of the elephant-hunters to look for the well, intending, if water was to be obtained, to rest here for the night. A pool was found, but the water was thick and muddy, and the negro discovered near it the remains of a fire recently extinguished, and the fragments of provisions, which afforded a proof that it had been lately visited, either by travellers or banditti. The fears of my attendants supposed the latter; and believing that robbers lurked near as, I was persuaded to change my resolution of resting here all night, and proceed to another watering-place, which I was assured we might reach early in the evening.

We departed accordingly, but it was eight o'clock at night before we came to the watering-place; and being now sufficiently fatigued with so long a day's journey, we kindled a large fire and lay down, surrounded by our cattle, on the bare ground, more than a gunshot from any bush, the negroes agreeing to keep watch by turns to prevent surprise.

I know not, indeed, that any danger was justly to be dreaded, but the negroes were unaccountably apprehensive of banditti during the whole of the journey. As soon, therefore, as daylight appeared, we filled our soofroos (skins) and calabashes at the pool, and set out for Tallika, the first town in Bondou, which we reached about eleven o'clock in the forenoon (the 13th of December).

CHAPTER IV

Tallika, the frontier town of Bondou towards Woolli, is inhabited chiefly by Foulahs of the Mohammedan religion, who live in considerable affluence, partly by furnishing provisions to the coffles, or caravans, that pass through the town, and partly by the sale of ivory, obtained by hunting elephants, in which employment the young men are generally very successful. Here an officer belonging to the king of Bondou constantly resides, whose business it is to give timely information of the arrival of the caravans, which are taxed according to the number of loaded asses that arrive at Tallika.

I took up my residence at this officer's house, and agreed with him to accompany me to Fatteconda, the residence of the king, for which he was to receive five bars; and before my departure I wrote a few lines to Dr. Laidley, and gave my letter to the master of a caravan bound for the Gambia. This caravan consisted of nine or ten people, with five asses loaded with ivory. The large teeth are conveyed in nets, two on each side of the ass; the small ones are wrapped up in skins, and secured with ropes.

December 14. - We left Tallika, and rode on very peaceably for about two miles, when a violent quarrel arose between two of my fellow-travellers, one of whom was the blacksmith, in the course of which they bestowed some opprobrious terms upon each other; and it is worthy of remark, that an African will sooner forgive a blow than a term of reproach applied to his ancestors. "Strike me, but do not curse my mother," is a common expression even among the slaves. This sort of abuse, therefore, so enraged one of the disputants, that he drew his cutlass upon the blacksmith, and would certainly have ended the dispute in a very serious manner, if the others had not laid hold of him and wrested the cutlass from him. I was obliged to interfere, and put an end to this disagreeable business by desiring the blacksmith to be silent, and telling the other, who I thought was in the wrong, that if he attempted in future to draw his cutlass, or molest any of my attendants, I should look upon him as a robber, and shoot him without further ceremony. This threat had the desired effect, and we marched sullenly along till the afternoon, when we arrived at a number of small villages scattered over an open and fertile plain. At one of these, called Ganado, we took up our residence for the night; here an exchange of presents and a good supper terminated all animosities among my attendants, and the night was far advanced before any of us thought of going to sleep. We were amused by an itinerant singing man, who told a number of diverting stories, and played some sweet airs by blowing his breath upon a bow-string, and striking it at the same time with a stick.

December 15. - At daybreak my fellow-travellers, the Serawoollies, took leave of me, with many prayers for my safety. About a mile from Ganado we crossed a considerable branch of the Gambia, called Neriko. The banks were steep and covered with mimosas; and I observed in the mud a number of large mussels, but the natives do not eat them. About noon, the sun being exceedingly hot, we rested two hours in the shade of a tree, and purchased some milk and pounded corn from some Foulah herdsmen, and at sunset reached a town called Koorkarany, where the blacksmith had some relations; and here we rested two days.

Koorkarany is a Mohammedan town surrounded by a high wall, and is provided with a mosque. Here I was shown a number of Arabic manuscripts, particularly a copy of the book before mentioned, called Al Sharra. The maraboo, or priest, in whose possession it was, read and explained to me in Mandingo many of the most remarkable passages, and, in return, I showed him Richardson's Arabic Grammar, which he very much admired.

On the evening of the second day (December 17) we departed from Koorkarany. We were joined by a young man who was travelling to Fatteconda for salt; and as night set in we reached Dooggi, a small village about three miles from Koorkarany.

Provisions were here so cheap that I purchased a bullock for six small stones of amber; for I found my company increase or diminish according to the good fare they met with.

December 18. - Early in the morning we departed from Dooggi, and, being joined by a number of Foulahs and other people, made a formidable appearance, and were under no apprehension of being plundered in the woods. About eleven o'clock, one of the asses proving very refractory, the negroes took a curious method to make him tractable. They cut a forked stick, and putting the forked part into the ass's mouth, like the bit of a bridle, tied the two smaller parts together above his head, leaving the lower part of the stick of sufficient length to strike against the ground, if the ass should attempt to put his head down. After this the ass walked along quietly and gravely enough, taking care, after some practice, to hold his head sufficiently high to prevent stones or roots of trees from striking against the end of the stick, which experience had taught him would give a severe shock to his teeth. This contrivance produced a ludicrous appearance, but my fellow-travellers told me it was constantly adopted by the slatees, and always proved effectual.

In the evening we arrived at a few scattered villages, surrounded with extensive cultivation, at one of which, called Buggil, we passed the night in a miserable hut, having no other bed than a bundle of corn-stalks, and no provisions but what we brought with us. The wells here are dug with great ingenuity, and are very deep. I measured one of the bucket-ropes, and found the depth of the well to be twenty-eight fathoms.

December 19. - We departed from Buggil, and travelled along a dry, stony height, covered with mimosas, till mid-day, when the land sloped towards the east, and we descended into a deep valley, in which I observed abundance of whinstone and white quartz. Pursuing our course to the eastward, along this valley in the bed of an exhausted river-course, we came to a large village, where we intended to lodge. We found many of the natives dressed in a thin French gauze, which they called byqui; this being a light airy dress, and well calculated to display the shape of their persons, is much esteemed by the ladies. The manners of these females, however, did not correspond with their dress, for they were rude and troublesome in the highest degree; they surrounded me in numbers, begging for amber, beads, andc., and were so vehement in their solicitations, that I found it impossible to resist them. They tore my cloak, cut the buttons from my boy's clothes, and were proceeding to other outrages, when I mounted my horse and rode off, followed for half-a-mile by a body of these harpies.

In the evening we reached Soobrudooka, and as my company was numerous (being fourteen), I purchased a sheep and abundance of corn for supper; after which we lay down by the bundles, and passed an uncomfortable night in a heavy dew.

December 20. - We departed from Soobrudooka, and at two o'clock reached a large village situated on the banks of the Falemé river, which is here rapid and rocky. The natives were employed in fishing in various ways. The large fish were taken in long baskets made of split cane, and placed in a strong current, which was created by walls of stone built across the stream, certain open places being left, through which the water rushed with great force. Some of these baskets were more than twenty feet long, and when once the fish had entered one of them, the force of the stream prevented it from returning. The small fish were taken in great numbers in hand-nets, which the natives weave of cotton, and use with great dexterity. The fish last mentioned are about the size of sprats, and are prepared for sale in different ways; the most common is by pounding them entire as they come from the stream, in a wooden mortar, and exposing them to dry in the sun, in large lumps like sugar loaves. It may be supposed that the smell is not very agreeable; but in the Moorish countries to the north of the Senegal, where fish is scarcely known, this preparation is esteemed as a luxury, and sold to considerable advantage. The manner of using it by the natives is by dissolving a piece of this black loaf in boiling water, and mixing it with their kouskous.

On returning to the village, after an excursion to the river-side to inspect the fishery, an old Moorish shereef came to bestow his blessing upon me, and beg some paper to write saphies upon.This man had seen Major Houghton in the kingdom of Kaarta, and told me that he died in the country of the Moors.

About three in the afternoon we continued our course along the bank of the river to the northward, till eight o'clock, when we reached Nayemow.Here the hospitable master of the town received us kindly, and presented us with a bullock.In return I gave him some amber and beads.

December 21. - In the morning, having agreed for a canoe to carry over my bundles, I crossed the river, which came up to my knees as I sat on my horse; but the water is so clear, that from the high bank the bottom is visible all the way over.

About noon we entered Fatteconda, the capital of Bondou, and in a little time received an invitation to the house of a respectable slatee: for as there are no public-houses in Africa, it is customary for strangers to stand at the bentang, or some other place of public resort, till they are invited to a lodging by some of the inhabitants.We accepted the offer; and in an hour afterwards a person came and told me that he was sent on purpose to conduct me to the king, who was very desirous of seeing me immediately, if I was not too much fatigued.

I took my interpreter with me, and followed the messenger till we got quite out of the town, and crossed some corn-fields; when, suspecting some trick, I stopped, and asked the guide whither he was going.Upon which, he pointed to a man sitting under a tree at some little distance, and told me that the king frequently gave audience in that retired manner, in order to avoid a crowd of people, and that nobody but myself and my interpreter must approach him.When I advanced the king desired me to come and sit by him upon the mat; and, after hearing my story, on which be made no observation, he asked if I wished to purchase any slaves or gold.Being answered in the negative, he seemed rather surprised, but desired me to come to him in the evening, and he would give me some provisions.

This monarch was called Almami, a Moorish name, though I was told that he was not a Mohammedan, but a kafir or pagan.I had heard that he had acted towards Major Houghton with great unkindness, and caused him to be plundered.His behaviour, therefore, towards myself at this interview, though much more civil than I expected, was far from freeing me from uneasiness.I still apprehended some double-dealing; and as I was now entirely in his power, I thought it best to smooth the way by a present.Accordingly, I took with me in the evening one canister of gunpowder, some amber, tobacco, and my umbrella; and as I considered that my bundles would inevitably be searched, I concealed some few articles in the roof of the hut where I lodged, and I put on my new blue coat in order to preserve it.

All the houses belonging to the king and his family are surrounded by a lofty mud wall, which converts the whole into a kind of citadel. The interior is subdivided into different courts. At the first place of entrance I observed a man standing with a musket on his shoulder; and I found the way to the presence very intricate, leading through many passages, with sentinels placed at the different doors. When we came to the entrance of the court in which the king resides, both my guide and interpreter, according to custom, took off their sandals; and the former pronounced the king's name aloud, repeating it till he was answered from within. We found the monarch sitting upon a mat, and two attendants with him. I repeated what I had before told him concerning the object of my journey, and my reasons for passing through his country. He seemed, however, but half satisfied. When I offered to show him the contents of my portmanteau, and everything belonging to me, he was convinced; and it was evident that his suspicion had arisen from a belief that every white man must of necessity be a trader. When I had delivered my presents, he seemed well pleased, and was particularly delighted with the umbrella, which he repeatedly furled and unfurled, to the great admiration of himself and his two attendants, who could not for some time comprehend the use of this wonderful machine. After this I was about to take my leave, when the king, desiring me to stop a while, began a long preamble in favour of the whites, extolling their immense wealth and good dispositions. He next proceeded to an eulogium on my blue coat, of which the yellow buttons seemed particularly to catch his fancy; and he concluded by entreating me to present him with it, assuring me, for my consolation under the loss of it, that he would wear it on all public occasions, and inform every one who saw it of my great liberality towards him. The request of an African prince, in his own dominions, particularly when made to a stranger, comes little short of a command. It is only a way of obtaining by gentle means what he can, if he pleases, take by force; and as it was against my interest to offend him by a refusal, I very quietly took off my coat, the only good one in my possession, and laid it at his feet.

In return for my compliance, he presented me with great plenty of provisions, and desired to see me again in the morning. I accordingly attended, and found in sitting upon his bed. He told me he was sick, and wished to have a little blood taken from him; but I had no sooner, tied up his arm and displayed the lancet, than his courage failed, and he begged me to postpone the operation till the afternoon, as he felt himself, he said, much better than he had been, and thanked me kindly for my readiness to serve him. He then observed that his women were very desirous to see me, and requested that I would favour them with a visit. An attendant was ordered to conduct me; and I had no sooner entered the court appropriated to the ladies, than the whole seraglio surrounded me - some begging for physic, some for amber, and all of them desirous of trying that great African specific, blood-letting. They were ten or twelve in number, most of them young and handsome, and wearing on their heads ornaments of gold, and beads of amber.

They rallied me with a good deal of gaiety on different subjects, particularly upon the whiteness of my skin and the prominency of my nose. They insisted that both were artificial. The first, they said, was produced when I was an infant, by dipping me in milk; and they insisted that my nose had been pinched every day, till it had acquired its present unsightly and unnatural conformation. On my part, without disputing my own deformity, I paid them many compliments on African beauty. I praised the glossy jet of their skins, and the lovely depression of their noses; but they said that flattery, or, as they emphatically termed it, honey-mouth, was not esteemed in Bondou. In return, however, for my company or my compliments (to which, by the way, they seemed not so insensible as they affected to be) they presented me with a jar of honey and some fish, which were sent to my lodging; and I was desired to come again to the king a little before sunset.

I carried with me some beads and writing-paper, it being usual to present some small offering on taking leave, in return for which the king gave me five drachms of gold, observing that it was but a trifle, and given out of pure friendship, but would be of use to me in travelling, for the purchase of provisions. He seconded this act of kindness by one still greater, politely telling me that, though it was customary to examine the baggage of every traveller passing through his country, yet, in the present instance, he would dispense without ceremony, adding, I was at liberty to depart when I pleased.

Accordingly, on the morning of the 23rd, we left Fatteconda, and about eleven o'clock came to a small village, where we determined to stop for the rest of the day.

In the afternoon my fellow-travellers informed me that, as this was the boundary between Bondou and Kajaaga, and dangerous for travellers, it would be necessary to continue our journey by night, until we should reach a more hospitable part of the country. I agreed to the proposal, and hired two people for guides through the woods; and as soon as the people of the village were gone to sleep (the moon shining bright) we set out. The stillness of the air, the howling of the wild beasts, and the deep solitude of the forest, made the scene solemn and oppressive. Not a word was uttered by any of us but in a whisper; all were attentive, and every one anxious to show his sagacity by pointing out to me the wolves and hyænas, as they glided like shadows from one thicket to another. Towards morning we arrived at a village called Kimmoo, where our guides awakened one of their acquaintances, and we stopped to give the asses some corn, and roast a few ground-nuts for ourselves. At daylight we resumed our journey, and in the afternoon arrived at Joag, in the kingdom of Kajaaga.

Being now in a country and among a people differing in many respects from those that have as yet fallen under our observation, I shall, before I proceed further, give some account of Bondou (the territory we have left) and its inhabitants, the Foulahs, the description of whom I purposely reserved for this part of my work.

Bondou is bounded on the east by Bambouk, on the south-east and south by Tenda and the Simbani wilderness, on the south-west by Woolli, on the west by Foota Torra, and on the north by Kajaaga.

The country, like that of Woolli, is very generally covered with woods, but the land is more elevated, and, towards the Falemé river, rises into considerable hills. In native fertility the soil is not surpassed, I believe, by any part of Africa.

From the central situation of Bondou, between the Gambia and Senegal rivers, it is become a place of great resort, both for the slatees, who generally pass through it on going from the coast to the interior countries, and for occasional traders, who frequently come hither from the inland countries to purchase salt.

These different branches of commerce are conducted principally by Mandingoes and Serawoollies, who have settled in the country. These merchants likewise carry on a considerable trade with Gedumah and other Moorish countries, bartering corn and blue cotton cloths for salt, which they again barter in Dentila and other districts for iron, shea-butter, and small quantities of gold-dust. They likewise sell a variety of sweet-smelling gums, packed up in small bags, containing each about a pound. These gums, being thrown on hot embers, produce a very pleasant odour, and are used by the Mandingoes for perfuming their huts and clothes.

The customs, or duties on travellers, are very heavy; in almost every town an ass-load pays a bar of European merchandise, and at Fatteconda, the residence of the king, one Indian baft, or a musket, and six bottles of gunpowder, are exacted as the common tribute. By means of these duties, the king of Bondou is well supplied with arms and ammunition - a circumstance which makes him formidable to the neighbouring states.

The inhabitants differ in their complexions and national manners from the Mandingoes and Serawoollies, with whom they are frequently at war. Some years ago the king of Bondou crossed the Falemé river with a numerous army; and, after a short and bloody campaign, totally defeated the forces of Samboo, king of Bambouk, who was obliged to sue for peace, and surrender to him all the towns along the eastern bank of the Falemé.

The Foulahs in general (as has been observed in a former chapter) are of a tawny complexion, with small features and soft silky hair; next to the Mandingoes, they are undoubtedly the most considerable of all the nations in this part of Africa. Their original country is said to be Fooladoo (which signifies the country of the Foulahs); but they possess at present many other kingdoms at a great distance from each other; their complexion, however, is not exactly the same in the different districts; in Bondou, and the other kingdoms which are situated in the vicinity of the Moorish territories, they are of a more yellow complexion than in the southern states.

The Foulahs of Bondou are naturally of a mild and gentle disposition, but the uncharitable maxims of the Koran have made them less hospitable to strangers, and more reserved in their behaviour, than the Mandingoes. They evidently consider all the negro natives as their inferiors; and, when talking of different nations, always rank themselves among the white people.

Their government differs from that of the Mandingoes chiefly in this, that they are more immediately under the influence of Mohammedan laws; for all the chief men, the king excepted, and a large majority of the inhabitants of Bondou, are Mussulmans, and the authority and laws of the Prophet are everywhere looked upon as sacred and decisive. In the exercise of their faith, however, they are not very intolerant towards such of their countrymen as still retain their ancient superstitions. Religious persecution is not known among them, nor is it necessary; for the system of Mohammed is made to extend itself by means abundantly more efficacious. By establishing small schools in the different towns, where many of the pagan as well as Mohammedan children are taught to read the Koran, and instructed in the tenets of the Prophet, the Mohammedan priests fix a bias on the minds, and form the character, of their young disciples, which no accidents of life can ever afterwards remove or alter. Many of these little schools I visited in my progress through the country, and I observed with pleasure the great docility and submissive deportment of the children, and heartily wished they had had better instructors and a purer religion.

With the Mohammedan faith is also introduced the Arabic language, with which most of the Foulahs have a slight acquaintance. Their native tongue abounds very much in liquids, but there is something unpleasant in the manner of pronouncing it. A stranger, on hearing the common conversation of two Foulahs, would imagine that they were scolding each other. Their numerals are these:-

One, Go.
Two, Deeddee.
Three, Tettee.
Four, Nee.
Five, Jouee.
Six, Jego.
Seven, Jedeeddee.
Eight, Je Tettee.
Nine, Je Nee.
Ten, Sappo.

The industry of the Foulahs, in the occupations of pasturage and agriculture, is everywhere remarkable. Even on the banks of the Gambia, the greater part of the corn is raised by them, and their herds and flocks are more numerous and in better condition than those of the Mandingoes; but in Bondou they are opulent in a high degree, and enjoy all the necessaries of life in the greatest profusion. They display great skill in the management of their cattle, making them extremely gentle by kindness and familiarity. On the approach of the night, they are collected from the woods and secured in folds called korrees, which are constructed in the neighbourhood of the different villages. In the middle of each korree is erected a small hut, wherein one or two of the herdsmen keep watch during the night, to prevent the cattle from being stolen, and to keep up the fires which are kindled round the korree to frighten away the wild beasts.

The cattle are milked in the mornings and evenings: the milk is excellent; but the quantity obtained from any one cow is by no means so great as in Europe. The Foulahs use the milk chiefly as an article of diet, and that not until it is quite sour. The cream which it affords is very thick, and is converted into butter by stirring it violently in a large calabash. This butter, when melted over a gentle fire, and freed from impurities, is preserved in small earthen pots, and forms a part in most of their dishes; it serves likewise to anoint their heads, and is bestowed very liberally on their faces and arms.

But although milk is plentiful, it is somewhat remarkable that the Foulahs, and indeed all the inhabitants of this part of Africa, are totally unacquainted with the art of making cheese. A firm attachment to the customs of their ancestors makes them view with an eye of prejudice everything that looks like innovation. The heat of the climate and the great scarcity of salt are held forth as unanswerable objections; and the whole process appears to them too long and troublesome to be attended with any solid advantage.

Besides the cattle, which constitute the chief wealth of the Foulahs, they possess some excellent horses, the breed of which seems to be a mixture of the Arabian with the original African.

CHAPTER V

The kingdom of Kajaaga, in which I was now arrived, is called by the French Gallam, but the name that I have adopted is universally used by the natives. This country is bounded on the south-east and south by Bambouk, on the west by Bondou and Foota-Torra, and on the north by the river Senegal.

The air and climate are, I believe, more pure and salubrious than at any of the settlements towards the coast; the face of the country is everywhere interspersed with a pleasing variety of hills and valleys; and the windings of the Senegal river, which descends from the rocky hills of the interior, make the scenery on its banks very picturesque and beautiful.

The inhabitants are called Serawoollies, or (as the French write it) Seracolets. Their complexion is a jet black: they are not to be distinguished in this respect from the Jaloffs.

The government is monarchical, and the regal authority, from what I experienced of it, seems to be sufficiently formidable. The people themselves, however, complain of no oppression, and seemed all very anxious to support the king in a contest he was going to enter into with the sovereign of Kasson. The Serawoollies are habitually a trading people; they formerly carried on a great commerce with the French in gold and slaves, and still maintain some traffic in slaves with the British factories on the Gambia. They are reckoned tolerably fair and just in their dealings, but are indefatigable in their exertions to acquire wealth, and they derive considerable profits by the sale of salt and cotton cloth in distant countries. When a Serawoolli merchant returns home from a trading expedition the neighbours immediately assemble to congratulate him upon his arrival. On these occasions the traveller displays his wealth and liberality by making a few presents to his friends; but if he has been unsuccessful his levee is soon over, and every one looks upon him as a man of no understanding, who could perform a long journey, and (at they express it) "bring back nothing but the hair upon his head."

Their language abounds much in gutturals, and is not so harmonious as that spoken by the Foulahs. It is, however, well worth acquiring by those who travel through this part of the African continent, it being very generally understood in the kingdoms of Kasson, Kaarta, Ludamar, and the northern parts of Bambarra. In all these countries the Serawoollies are the chief traders. Their numerals are:-

One, Bani.
Two, Fillo.
Three, Sicco.
Four, Narrato.
Five, Karrago.
Six, Toomo.
Seven, Nero.
Eight, Sego.
Nine, Kabbo.
Ten, Tamo.
Twenty, Tamo di Fillo.

We arrived at Joag, the frontier town of this kingdom, on the 24th of December, and took up our residence at the house of the chief man, who is here no longer known by the title of alkaid, but is called the dooty. He was a rigid Mohammedan, but distinguished for his hospitality. This town may be supposed, on a gross computation, to contain two thousand inhabitants. It is surrounded by a high wall, in which are a number of port-holes, for musketry to fire through, in case of an attack. Every man's possession is likewise surrounded by a wall, the whole forming so many distinct citadels; and amongst a people unacquainted with the use of artillery these walls answer all the purposes of stronger fortifications. To the westward of the town is a small river, on the banks of which the natives raise great plenty of tobacco and onions.

The same evening Madiboo, the bushreen, who had accompanied me from Pisania, went to pay a visit to his father and mother, who dwelt at a neighbouring town called Dramanet. He was joined by my other attendant, the blacksmith. As soon as it was dark I was invited to see the sports of the inhabitants, it being their custom, on the arrival of strangers, to welcome them by diversions of different kinds. I found a great crowd surrounding a party who were dancing, by the light of some large fires, to the music of four drums, which were beat with great exactness and uniformity. The dances, however, consisted more in wanton gestures than in muscular exertion or graceful attitudes. The ladies vied with each other in displaying the most voluptuous movements imaginable.

December 25. - About two o'clock in the morning a number of horsemen came into the town, and, having awakened my landlord, talked to him for some time in the Serawoolli tongue; after which they dismounted and came to the bentang, on which I had made my bed. One of them, thinking that I was asleep, attempted to steal the musket that lay by me on the mat, but finding that he could not effect his purpose undiscovered, he desisted, and the strangers sat down by me till daylight.

I could now easily perceive, by the countenance of my interpreter, Johnson, that something very unpleasant was in agitation. I was likewise surprised to see Madiboo and the blacksmith so soon returned. On inquiring the reason, Madiboo informed me that, as they were dancing at Dramanet, ten horsemen belonging to Batcheri, king of the country, with his second son at their head, had arrived there, inquiring if the white man had passed, and, on being told that I was at Joag, they rode off without stopping. Madiboo added that on hearing this he and the blacksmith hastened back to give me notice of their coming. Whilst I was listening to this narrative the ten horsemen mentioned by Madiboo arrived, and coming to the bentang, dismounted and seated themselves with those who had come before - the whole being about twenty in number - forming a circle round me, and each man holding his musket in his hand. I took this opportunity to observe to my landlord that, as I did not understand the Serawoolli tongue, I hoped whatever the men had to say they would speak in Mandingo. To this they agreed; and a short man, loaded with a remarkable number of saphies, opened the business in a very long harangue, informing me that I had entered the king's town without having first paid the duties, or giving any present to the king; and that, according to the laws of the country, my people, cattle, and baggage were forfeited. He added that they had received orders from the king to conduct me to Maana, {2} the place of his residence, and if I refused to come with them their orders were to bring me by force; upon his saying which all of them rose up and asked me if I was ready. It would have been equally vain and imprudent in me to have resisted or irritated such a body of men; I therefore affected to comply with their commands, and begged them only to stop a little until I had given my horse a feed of corn, and settled matters with my landlord. The poor blacksmith, who was a native of Kasson, mistook this feigned compliance for a real intention, and taking me away from the company, told me that he had always behaved towards me as if I had been his father and master, and he hoped I would not entirely ruin him by going to Maana, adding that as there was every reason to believe a war would soon take place between Kasson and Kajaaga, he should not only lose his little property, the savings of four years' industry, but should certainly be detained and sold as a slave, unless his friends had an opportunity of paying two slaves for his redemption. I saw this reasoning in its full force, and determined to do my utmost to preserve the blacksmith from so dreadful a fate. I therefore told the king's son that I was ready to go with him, upon condition that, the blacksmith, who was an inhabitant of a distant kingdom, and entirely unconnected with me, should be allowed to stay at Joag till my return. To this they all objected, and insisted that, as we had all acted contrary to the laws, we were all equally answerable for our conduct.

I now took my landlord aside, and giving him a small present of gunpowder, asked his advice in such critical a situation. He was decidedly of opinion that I ought not to go to the king: he was fully convinced, he said, that if the king should discover anything valuable in my possession, he would not be over scrupulous about the means of obtaining it.

Towards the evening, as I was sitting upon the bentang chewing straws, an old female slave, passing by with a basket upon her head, asked me if had got my dinner. As I thought she only laughed at me, I gave her no answer; but my boy, who was sitting close by, answered for me, and told her that the king's people had robbed me of all my money. On hearing this, the good old woman, with a look of unaffected benevolence, immediately took the basket from her head, and showing me that it contained ground nuts, asked me if I could eat them. Being answered in the affirmative, she presented me with a few handfuls, and walked away before I had time to thank her for this seasonable supply.

The old woman had scarcely left me when I received information that a nephew of Demba Sego Jalla, the Mandingo king of Kasson, was coming to pay me a visit. He had been sent on an embassy to Batcheri, King of

Kajaaga, to endeavour to settle the disputes which had arisen between his uncle and the latter; but after debating the matter four days without success, he was now on his return, and hearing that a white man was at Joag, on his way to Kasson, curiosity brought in to see me. I represented to him my situation and distresses, when he frankly offered me his protection, and said he would be my guide to Kasson (provided I would set out the next morning), and be answerable for my safety. I readily and gratefully accepted his offer, and was ready with my attendants by daylight on the morning of the 27th of December.

My protector, whose name was Demba Sego, probably after his uncle, had a numerous retinue. Our company, at leaving Joag, consisted of thirty persons and six loaded asses; and we rode on cheerfully enough for some hours, without any remarkable occurrence until we came to a species of tree for which my interpreter Johnson had made frequent inquiry. On finding it, he desired us to stop, and producing a white chicken, which he had purchased at Joag for the purpose, he tied it by the leg to one of the branches, and then told us we might now safely proceed, for that our journey would be prosperous.

At noon we had reached Gungadi, a large town where we stopped about an hour, until some of the asses that had fallen behind came up. Here I observed a number of date-trees, and a mosque built of clay, with six turrets, on the pinnacles of which were placed six ostrich eggs. A little before sunset we arrived at the town of Samee, on the banks of the Senegal, which is here a beautiful but shallow river, moving slowly over a bed of sand and gravel. The banks are high, and covered with verdure - the country is open and cultivated - and the rocky hills of Fellow and Bambouk add much to the beauty of the landscape.

December 28. - We departed from Samee, and arrived in the afternoon at Kayee, a large village, part of which is situated on the north and part on the south side of the river.

The ferryman then taking hold of the most steady of the horses by a rope, led him into the water, and paddled the canoe a little from the brink; upon which a general attack commenced upon the other horses, who, finding themselves pelted and kicked on all sides, unanimously plunged into the river, and followed their companion. A few boys swam in after them; and, by laving water upon them when they attempted to return, urged them onwards; and we had the satisfaction in about fifteen minutes to see them all safe on the other side. It was a matter of greater difficulty to manage the asses; their natural stubbornness of disposition made them endure a great deal of pelting and shoving before they would venture into the water; and when they had reached the middle of the stream, four of them turned back, in spite of every exertion to get them forwards. Two hours were spent in getting the whole of them over; an hour more was employed in transporting the baggage; and it was near sunset before the canoe returned, when Demba Sego and myself embarked in this dangerous passage-boat, which the least motion was like to overset. The king's nephew thought this a proper time to have a peep into a tin box of mine that stood in the fore part of the canoe; and in stretching out his band for it, he unfortunately destroyed the equilibrium, and overset the canoe. Luckily we were not far advanced, and got back to the shore without much difficulty; from whence, after wringing the water from our clothes, we took a fresh departure, and were soon afterwards safely landed in Kasson.

CHAPTER VI

We no sooner found ourselves safe in Kasson than Demba Sego told me that we were now in his uncle's dominions, and he hoped I would consider, being now out of danger, the obligation I owed to him, and make him a suitable return for the trouble he had taken on my account by a handsome present. This, as he knew how much had been pilfered from me at Joag, was rather an unexpected proposition, and I began to fear that I had not much improved my condition by crossing the water; but as it would have been folly to complain I made no observation upon his conduct, and gave him seven bars of amber and some tobacco, with which he seemed to be content.

After a long day's journey, in the course of which I observed a number of large loose nodules of white granite, we arrived at Teesee on the evening of December 29th, and were accommodated in Demba Sego's hut. The next morning he introduced me to his father, Tiggity Sego, brother to the king of Kasson, chief of Teesee. The old man viewed me with great earnestness, having never, he said, beheld but one white man before, whom by his description I immediately knew to be Major Houghton.

In the afternoon one of his slaves eloped; and a general alarm being given, every person that had a horse rode into the woods, in the hopes of apprehending him, and Demba Sego begged the use of my horse for the same purpose. I readily consented; and in about an hour they all returned with the slave, who was severely flogged, and afterwards put in irons. On the day following (December 31st) Demba Sego was ordered to go with twenty horsemen to a town in Gedumah, to adjust some dispute with the Moors, a party of whom were supposed to have stolen three horses from Teesee. Demba begged a second the time use of my horse, adding that the sight of my bridle and saddle would give him consequence among the Moors. This request also I readily granted, and he promised to return at the end of three days. During his absence I amused myself with walking about the town, and conversing with the natives, who attended me everywhere with great kindness and curiosity, and supplied me with milk, eggs, and what other provisions I wanted, on very easy terms.

Teesee is a large unwalled town, having no security against the attack of an enemy except a sort of citadel in which Tiggity and his family constantly reside.This town, according to the report of the natives, was formerly inhabited only by a few Foulah shepherds, who lived in considerable affluence by means of the excellent meadows in the neighbourhood, in which they reared great herds of cattle.But their prosperity attracting the envy of some Mandingoes, the latter drove out the shepherds, and took possession of their lands.

The present inhabitants, though they possess both cattle and corn in abundance, are not over nice in articles of diet; rats, moles, squirrels, snakes, locusts, are eaten without scruple by the highest and lowest.My people were one evening invited to a feast given by some of the townsmen, where, after making a hearty meal of what they thought fish and kouskous, one of them found a piece of hard skin in the dish, and brought it along with him to show me what sort of fish they had been eating.On examining the skin I found they had been feasting on a large snake.Another custom still more extraordinary is that no woman is allowed to eat an egg.This prohibition, whether arising from ancient superstition or from the craftiness of some old bushreen who loved eggs himself, is rigidly adhered to, and nothing will more affront a woman of Teesee than to offer her an egg.The custom is the more singular, as the men eat eggs without scruple in the presence of their wives, and I never observed the same prohibition in any other of the Mandingo countries.

The third day after his son's departure, Tiggity Sego held a palaver on a very extraordinary occasion, which I attended; and the debates on both sides of the question displayed much ingenuity.The case was this:- A young man, a kafir of considerable affluence, who had recently married a young and handsome wife, applied to a very devout bushreen, or Mussalman priest, of his acquaintance, to procure him saphies for his protection during the approaching war.The bushreen complied with the request; and in order, as he pretended, to render the saphies more efficacious, enjoined the young man to avoid any nuptial intercourse with his bride for the space of six weeks.Severe as the injunction was, the kafir strictly obeyed; and, without telling his wife the real cause, absented himself from her company.In the meantime, it began to be whispered at Teesee that the bushreen, who always performed his evening devotions at the door of the kafir's hut, was more intimate with the young wife than he ought to be.At first the good husband was unwilling to suspect the honour of his sanctified friend, and one whole month elapsed before any jealousy rose in his mind, but hearing the charge repeated, he at last interrogated his wife on the subject, who frankly confessed that the bushreen had seduced her.Hereupon the kafir put her into confinement, and called a palaver upon the bushreen's conduct. The fact was clearly proved against him; and he was sentenced to be sold into slavery, or to find two slaves for his redemption, according to the pleasure of the complainant. The injured husband, however, was unwilling to proceed against his friend to such extremity, and desired rather to have him publicly flogged before Tiggity Sego's gate. This was agreed to, and the sentence was immediately executed. The culprit was tied by the hands to a strong stake; and a long black rod being brought forth, the executioner, after flourishing it round his head for some time, applied it with such force and dexterity to the bushreen's back as to make him roar until the woods resounded with his screams. The surrounding multitude, by their hooting and laughing, manifested how much they enjoyed the punishment of this old gallant; and it is worthy of remark that the number of stripes was precisely the same as are enjoined by the Mosaic law, forty, save one.

As there appeared great probability that Teesee, from its being a frontier town, would be much exposed during the war to the predatory incursions of the Moors of Gedumah, Tiggity Sego had, before my arrival, sent round to the neighbouring villages to beg or to purchase as much provisions as would afford subsistence to the inhabitants for one whole year, independently of the crop on the ground, which the Moors might destroy. This project was well received by the country people, and they fixed a day on which to bring all the provisions they could spare to Teesee; and as my horse was not yet returned, I went, in the afternoon of January 4th, 1796, to meet the escort with the provisions.

It was composed of about 400 men, marching in good order, with corn and ground nuts in large calabashes upon their heads. They were preceded by a strong guard of bowmen, and followed by eight musicians or singing men. As soon as they approached the town the latter began a song, every verse of which was answered by the company, and succeeded by a few strokes on the large drums. In this manner they proceeded, amidst the acclamations of the populace, till they reached the house of Tiggity Sego, where the loads were deposited; and in the evening they all assembled under the bentang tree, and spent the night in dancing and merriment.

On the 5th of January an embassy of ten people belonging to Almami Abdulkader, king of Foota-Torra, a country to the west of Bondou, arrived at Teesee; and desiring Tiggity to call an assembly of the inhabitants, announced publicly their king's determination to this effect:- 'That unless all the people of Kasson would embrace the Mohammedan religion, and evince their conversion by saying eleven public prayers, he, the king of Foota-Torra, could not possibly stand neuter in the present contest, but would certainly join his arms to those of Kajaaga.' A message of this nature from so powerful a prince could not fail to create great alarm; and the inhabitants of Teesee, after a long consultation, agreed to conform to his good pleasure, humiliating as it was to them. Accordingly, one and all publicly offered up eleven prayers, which were considered a sufficient testimony of their having renounced paganism, and embraced the doctrines of the prophet.

It was time 8th of January before Demba Sego returned with my horse; and being quite wearied out with the delay, I went immediately to inform his father that I should set out for Kooniakary early the next day. The old man made many frivolous objections, and at length gave me to understand that I must not think of departing without first paying him the same duties he was entitled to receive from all travellers; besides which he expected, he said, some acknowledgment for his kindness towards use. Accordingly, on the morning of the 9th, my friend Demba, with a number of people, came to me, and said that they were sent by Tiggity Sego for my present, and wished to see what goods I had appropriated for that purpose. I knew that resistance was hopeless, and complaint unavailing: and being in some measure prepared by the intimation I had received the night before, I quietly offered him seven bars of amber and five of tobacco. After surveying these articles for some time very coolly, Demba laid them down, and told me that this was not a present for a man of Tiggity Sego's consequence, who had it in his power to take whatever he pleased from me. He added, that if I did not consent to make him a larger offering he would carry all my baggage to his father, and let him choose for himself. I had no time for reply, for Demba and his attendants immediately began to open my bundles, and spread the different articles upon the floor, where they underwent a more strict examination than they had done at Joag. Everything that pleased them they took without scruple: and amongst other things, Demba seized the tin box that had so much attracted his attention in crossing the river. Upon collecting the scattered remains of my little fortune after these people had left me, I found that, as at Joag I had been plundered of half, so here, without even the shadow of accusation, I was deprived of half the remainder. The blacksmith himself, though a native of Kasson, had also been compelled to open his bundles, and take an oath that the different articles they contained were his own exclusive property. There was, however, no remedy, and having been under some obligation to Demba Sego for his attention towards me in the journey from Joag, I did not reproach him for his rapacity, but determined to quit Teesee, at all events, the next morning. In the meanwhile, in order to raise the drooping spirits of my attendants, I purchased a fat sheep, and had it dressed for our dinner.

Early in the morning of January 10th, therefore, I left Teesee, and about mid-day ascended a ridge, from whence we had a distant view of the hills round Kooniakary. In the evening we reached a small village, where we slept, and, departing from thence the next morning, crossed in a few hours a narrow but deep stream called Krieko, a branch of the Senegal. About two miles farther to the eastward we passed a large town called Madina, and at two o'clock came in sight of Jumbo, the blacksmith's native town, from whence he had been absent more than four years.Soon after this, his brother, who had by some means been apprised of his coming, came out to meet him, accompanied by a singing man.He brought a horse for the blacksmith, that he might enter his native town in a dignified manner; and he desired each of us to put a good charge of powder into our guns.The singing man now led the way, followed by the two brothers, and we were presently joined by a number of people from the town, all of whom demonstrated great joy at seeing their old acquaintance the blacksmith by the most extravagant jumping and singing.On entering the town the singing man began an extempore song in praise of the blacksmith, extolling his courage in having overcome so many difficulties, and concluding with a strict injunction to his friends to dress him plenty of victuals.

When we arrived at the blacksmith's place of residence we dismounted, and fired our muskets.The meeting between him and his relations was very tender; for these rude children of nature, free from restraint, display their emotions in the strongest and most expressive manner.Amidst these transports the blacksmith's aged mother was led forth, leaning upon a staff.Every one made way for her, and she stretched out her hand to bid her son welcome.Being totally blind, she stroked his hands, arms, and face with great care, and seemed highly delighted that her latter days were blessed by his return, and that her ears once more heard the music of his voice.

During the tumult of these congratulations I had seated myself apart by the side of one of the huts, being unwilling to interrupt the flow of filial and parental tenderness; and the attention of the company was so entirely taken up with the blacksmith that I believe none of his friends had observed me.When all the people present had seated themselves the blacksmith was desired by his father to give them some account of his adventures; and silence being commanded, he began, and after repeatedly thanking God for the success that had attended him, related every material occurrence that had happened to him from his leasing Kasson to his arrival at the Gambia, his employment and success in those parts, and the dangers he had escaped in returning to his native country.In the latter part of his narration he had frequently occasion to mention me; and after many strong expressions concerning my kindness to him he pointed to the place where I sat, and exclaimed, "Affille ibi siring!" - ("See him sitting there!")In a moment all eyes were turned upon me; I appeared like a being dropped from the clouds; every one was surprised that they had not observed me before; and a few women and children expressed great uneasiness at being so near a man of such an uncommon appearance.

By degrees, however, their apprehensions subsided, and when the blacksmith assured them that I was perfectly inoffensive, and would hurt nobody, some of them ventured so far as to examine the texture of my clothes; but many of them were still very suspicious; and when by accident I happened to move myself, or look at the young children, their mothers would scamper off with them with the greatest precipitations.In a few hours, however, they all because reconciled to me.

With these worthy people I spent the remainder of that and the whole of the ensuing day, in feasting and merriment; and the blacksmith declared he would not quit me during my stay at Kooniakary - for which place we set out early on the morning of the 14th of January, and arrived about the middle of the day at Soolo, a small village three miles to the south of it.

As this place was somewhat out of the direct road, it is necessary to observe that I went thither to visit a slatee or Gambia trader, of great note and reputation, named Salim Daucari.He was well known to Dr. Laidley, who had trusted him with effects to the value of five slaves, and had given me an order for the whole of the debt.We luckily found him at home, and he received me with great kindness and attention.

It is remarkable, however, that the king of Kasson was by some means immediately apprised of my motions; for I had been at Soolo but a few hours before Sambo Sego, his second son, came thither with a party of horse, to inquire what had prevented me from proceeding to Kooniakary, and waiting immediately upon the king, who, he said, was impatient to see me.Salim Daucari made my apology, and promised to accompany me to Kooniakary the same evening.We accordingly departed from Soolo at sunset, and in about an hour entered Kooniakary.But as the king had gone to sleep we deferred the interview till next morning, and slept at the hut of Sambo Sego.

CHAPTER VII

About eight o'clock in the morning of January 15th, 1796, we went to an audience of the king (Demba Sego Jalla), but the crowd of people to see me was so great that I could scarcely get admittance.A passage being at length obtained, I made my bow to the monarch, whom we found sitting upon a mat, in a large hut.He appeared to be a man of about sixty years of age.His success in war, and the mildness of his behaviour in time of peace, had much endeared him to all his subjects.He surveyed me with great attention; and when Salim Daucari explained to him the object of my journey, and my reasons for passing through his country, the good old king appeared not only perfectly satisfied, but promised me every assistance in his power.He informed me that he had seen Major Houghton, and presented him with a white horse; but that, after crossing the kingdom of Kaarta, he had lost his life among the Moors, in what manner he could not inform me.When this audience was ended we returned to our lodging, and I made up a small present for the king out of the few effects that were left me; for I had not yet received anything from Salim Daucari.This present, though inconsiderable in itself, was well received by the king, who sent me in return a large white bullock.The sight of this animal quite delighted my attendants; not so much on account of its bulk, as from its being of a white colour, which is considered as a particular mark of favour.But although the king himself was well disposed towards me, and readily granted me permission to pass through his territories, I soon discovered that very great and unexpected obstacles were likely to impede my progress.Besides the war which was on the point of breaking out between Kasson and Kajaaga, I was told that the next kingdom of Kaarta, through which my route lay, was involved in the issue, and was furthermore threatened with hostilities on the part of Bambarra.The king himself informed me of these circumstances, and advised me to stay in the neighbourhood of Kooniakary till such time as he could procure proper information respecting Bambarra, which he expected to do in the course of four or five days, as he had already, he said, sent four messengers into Kaarta for that purpose.I readily submitted to this proposal, and went to Soolo, to stay there till the return of one of those messengers.This afforded me a favourable opportunity of receiving what money Salim Daucari could spare me on Dr. Laidley's account.I succeeded in receiving the value of there slaves, chiefly in gold dust; and being anxious to proceed as quickly as possible, I begged Daucari to use his interest with the king to allow me a guide by the way of Fooladoo, as I was informed that the war had already commenced between the kings of Bambarra and Kaarta.Daucari accordingly set out for Kooniakary on the morning of the 20th, and the same evening returned with the king's answer, which was to this purpose - that the king had, many years ago, made an agreement with Daisy, king of Kaarta, to send all merchants and travellers through his dominions; but that if I wished to take the route through Fooladoo I had his permission so to do; though he could not, consistently with his agreement, lend me a guide.Having felt the want of regal protection in a former part of my journey, I was unwilling to hazard a repetition of the hardships I had then experienced, especially as the money I had received was probably the last supply that I should obtain.I therefore determined to wait for the return of the messengers from Kaarta.

In the interim it began to be whispered abroad that I had received plenty of gold from Salim Daucari, and, on the morning of the 23rd, Sambo Sego paid me a visit, with a party of horsemen.He insisted upon knowing the exact amount of the money I had obtained, declaring that whatever the sum was, one-half of it must go to the king; besides which he intimated that he expected a handsome present for himself, as being the king's son, and for his attendants, as being the king's relations.I prepared to submit; and if Salim Daucari had not interposed all my endeavours to mitigate this oppressive claim would have been of no avail.Salim at last prevailed upon Sambo to accept sixteen bars of European merchandise, and some powder and ball, as a complete payment of every demand that could be made upon me in the kingdom of Kasson.

January 26. - In the forenoon I went to the top of a high hill to the southward of Soolo, where I had a most enchanting prospect of the country.The number of towns and villages, and the extensive cultivation around them, surpassed everything I had yet seen in Africa.A gross calculation may be formed of the number of inhabitants in this delightful plain by considering that the king of Kasson can raise four thousand fighting men by the sound of his war-drum.In traversing the rocky eminences of this hill, which are almost destitute of vegetation, I observed a number of large holes in the crevasses and fissures of the rocks, where the wolves and hyænas take refuge during the day.

February 1. - The messengers arrived from Kaarta, and brought intelligence that the war had not yet commenced between Bambarra and Kaarta, and that I might probably pass through Kaarta before the Bambarra army invaded that country.

February 3. - Early in the morning two guides on horseback came from Kooniakary to conduct me to the frontiers of Kaarta.I accordingly took leave of Salim Daucari, and parted for the last time from my fellow-traveller the blacksmith, whose kind solicitude for my welfare had been so conspicuous, and about ten o'clock departed from Soolo.We travelled this day through a rocky and hilly country, along the banks of the river Krieko, and at sunset came to the village of Soomo, where we slept.

February 4. - We departed from Soomo, and continued our route along the banks of the Krieko, which are everywhere well cultivated, and swarm with inhabitants.At this time they were increased by the number of people that had flown thither from Kaarta on account of the Bambarra war.In the afternoon we reached Kimo, a large village, the residence of Madi Konko, governor of the hilly country of Kasson, which is called Sorroma.From hence the guides appointed by the king of Kasson returned, to join in the expedition against Kajaaga; and I waited until the 6th before I could prevail on Madi Konko to appoint me a guide to Kaarta.

February 7. - Departing from Kimo, with Madi Konko's son as a guide, we continued our course along the banks of the Krieko until the afternoon, when we arrived at Kangee, a considerable town.The Krieko is here but a small rivulet.This beautiful stream takes its rise a little to the eastward of this town, and descends with a rapid and noisy current until it reaches the bottom of the high hill called Tappa, where it becomes more placid, and winds gently through the lovely plains of Kooniakary; after which, having received an additional branch from the north, it is lost in the Senegal, somewhere near the falls of Felow.

February 8. - This day we travelled over a rough stony country, and having passed Seimpo and a number of other villages, arrived in the afternoon at Lackarago, a small village which stands upon the ridge of hills that separates the kingdoms of Kasson and Kaarta. In the course of the day we passed many hundreds of people flying from Kaarta with their families and effects.

February 9. - Early in the morning we departed from Lackarago, and a little to the eastward came to the brow of a hill from whence we had an extensive view of the country. Towards the south-east were perceived some very distant hills, which our guide told us were the mountains of Fooladoo. We travelled with great difficulty down a stony and abrupt precipice, and continued our way in the bed of a dry river course, where the trees, meeting overhead, made the place dark and cool. In a little time we reached the bottom of this romantic glen, and about ten o'clock emerged from between two rocky hills, and found ourselves on the level and sandy plains of Kaarta. At noon we arrived at a korree, or watering place, where for a few strings of beads I purchased as much milk and corn-meal as we could eat; indeed, provisions are here so cheap, and the shepherds live in such affluence, that they seldom ask any return for what refreshments a traveller receives from them. From this korree we reached Feesurah at sunset, where we took up our lodging for the night.

February 10. - We continued at Feesurah all this day, to have a few clothes washed, and learn more exactly the situation of affairs before we ventured towards the capital.

February 11 - Our landlord, taking advantage of the unsettled state of the country, demanded so extravagant a sum for our lodging that, suspecting he wished for an opportunity to quarrel with us, I refused to submit to his exorbitant demand; but my attendants were so much frightened at the reports of approaching war that they refused to proceed any farther unless I could settle matters with him, and induce him to accompany us to Kemoo, for our protection on the road. This I accomplished with some difficulty; and by a present of a blanket which I had brought with me to sleep in, and for which our landlord had conceived a very great liking, matters were at length amicably adjusted, and he mounted his horse and led the way. He was one of those negroes who, together with the ceremonial part of the Mohammedan religion, retain all their ancient superstitions, and even drink strong liquors. They are called Johars, or Jowars, and in this kingdom form a very numerous and powerful tribe. We had no sooner got into a dark need lonely part of the first wood than he made a sign for us to stop, and, taking hold of a hollow piece of bamboo that hung as an amulet round his neck, whistled very loud there times. I confess I was somewhat startled, thinking it was a signal for some of his companions to come and attack us; but he assured me that it was done merely with a view to ascertain what success we were likely to meet with on our present journey. He then dismounted, laid his spear across the road, and having said a number of short prayers, concluded with three loud whistles; after which he listened for some time, as if in expectation of an answer, and receiving none, told us we might proceed without fear, for there was no danger. About noon we passed a number of large villages quite deserted, the inhabitants having fled into Kasson to avoid the horrors of war. We reached Karankalla at sunset. This formerly was a large town, but having been plundered by the Bambarrans about four years ago, nearly one-half of it is still in ruins.

February 12. - At daylight we departed from Karankalla, and as it was but a short day's journey to Kemmoo, we travelled slower than usual, and amused ourselves by collecting such eatable fruits as grew near the roadside. About noon we saw at a distance the capital of Kaarta, situated in the middle of an open plain - the country for two miles round being cleared of wood, by the great consumption of that article for building and fuel - and we entered the town about two o'clock in the afternoon.

We proceeded without stopping to the court before the king's residence; but I was so completely surrounded by the gazing multitude that I did not attempt to dismount, but sent in the landlord and Madi Konki's son, to acquaint the king of my arrival. In a little time they returned, accompanied by a messenger from the king, signifying that he would see me in the evening; and in the meantime the messenger had orders to procure me a lodging and see that the crowd did not molest me. He conducted me into a court, at the door of which he stationed a man with a stick in his hand to keep off the mob, and then showed me a large hut in which I was to lodge. I had scarcely seated myself in this spacious apartment when the mob entered; it was found impossible to keep them out, and I was surrounded by as many as the hut could contain. When the first party, however, had seen me, and asked a few questions, they retired to make room for another company; and in this manner the hut was filled and emptied thirteen different times.

A little before sunset the king sent to inform me that he was at leisure, and wished to see me. I followed the messenger through a number of courts surrounded with high walls, where I observed plenty of dry grass, bundled up like hay, to fodder the horses, in case the town should be invested. On entering the court in which the king was sitting I was astonished at the number of his attendants, and at the good order that seemed to prevail among them; they were all seated - the fighting men on the king's right hand and the women and children on the left, leaving a space between them for my passage. The king, whose name was Daisy Koorabarri, was not to be distinguished from his subjects by any superiority in point of dress; a bank of earth, about two feet high, upon which was spread a leopard's skin, constituted the only mark of royal dignity. When I had seated myself upon the ground before him, and related the various circumstances that had induced me to pass through his country, and my reasons for soliciting his protections, he appeared perfectly satisfied; but said it was not in his power at present to afford me much assistance, for that all sort of communication between Kaarta and Bambarra had been interrupted for some time past; and as Mansong, the king of Bambarra, with his army, had entered Fooladoo in his way to Kaarta, there was but little hope of my reaching Bambarra by any of the usual routes, inasmuch as, coming from an enemy's country, I should certainly be plundered, or taken for a spy. If his country had been at peace, he said, I might have remained with him until a more favourable opportunity offered; but, as matters stood at present, he did not wish me to continue in Kaarta, for fear some accident should befall me, in which case my countrymen might say that he had murdered a white man. He would therefore advise me to return into Kasson, and remain there until the war should terminate, which would probably happen in the course of three or four months, after which, if he was alive, he said, he would be glad to see me, and if he was dead his sons would take care of me.

This advice was certainly well meant on the part of the king, and perhaps I was to blame in not following it; but I reflected that the hot months were approaching, and I dreaded the thoughts of spending the rainy season in the interior of Africa. These considerations, and the aversion I felt at the idea of returning without having made a greater progress in discovery, made sue determine to go forward; and though the king could not give me a guide to Bambarra, I begged that he would allow a man to accompany me as near the frontiers of his kingdom as was consistent with safety. Finding that I was determined to proceed, the king told me that one route still remained, but that, he said, was by no means free from danger - which was to go from Kaarta into the Moorish kingdom of Ludamar, from whence I might pass by a circuitous route into Bambarra. If I wished to follow this route he would appoint people to conduct me to Jarra, the frontier town of Ludamar. He then inquired very particularly how I had been treated since I had left the Gambia, and asked, in a jocular way, how many slaves I expected to carry home with me on my return. He was about to proceed when a man mounted on a fine Moorish horse, which was covered with sweat and foam, entered the court, and signifying that he had something of importance to communicate, the king immediately took up his sandals, which is the signal to strangers to retire. I accordingly took leave, but desired my boy to stay about the place, in order to learn something of the intelligence that this messenger had brought. In about an hour the boy returned, and informed me that the Bambarra army had left Fooladoo, and was on its march towards Kaarta; that the man I had seen, who had brought this intelligence, was one of the scouts, or watchmen, employed by the king, each of whom has his particular station (commonly on some rising ground) from whence he has the best view of the country, and watches the motions of the enemy.

February 13. - At daylight I sent my horse-pistols and holsters as a present to the king, and being very desirous to get away from a place which was likely soon to become the seat of war, I begged the messenger to inform the king that I wished to depart from Kemmoo as soon as he should find it convenient to appoint me a guide.In about an hour the king sent his messenger to thank me for the present, and eight horsemen to conduct me to Jarra.They told me that the king wished me to proceed to Jarra with all possible expedition, that they might return before anything decisive should happen between the armies of Bambarra need Kaarta.We accordingly departed forthwith from Kemmoo, accompanied by three of Daisy's sons, and about two hundred horsemen, who kindly undertook to see me a little way on my journey.

CHAPTER VIII

On the evening of the day of our departure from Kemmoo (the king's eldest son and great part of the horsemen having returned) we reached a village called Marina, where we slept.During the night some thieves broke into the hut where I had deposited my baggage, and having cut open one of my bundles, stole a quantity of beads, part of my clothes, and some amber and gold, which happened to be in one of the pockets.I complained to my protectors, but without effect.The next day (February 14th) was far advanced before we departed from Marina, and we travelled slowly, on account of the excessive heat, until four o'clock in the afternoon, when two negroes were observed sitting among some thorny bushes, at a little distance from the road.The king's people, taking it for granted that they were runaway slaves, cocked their muskets, and rode at full speed in different directions through the bushes, in order to surround them, and prevent their escaping.The negroes, however, waited with great composure until we came within bowshot of them, when each of them took from his quiver a handful of arrows, and putting two between his teeth and one in his bow, waved to us with his hand to keep at a distance; upon which one of the king's people called out to the strangers to give some account of themselves.They said that "they were natives of Toorda, a neighbouring village, and had come to that place to gather tomberongs."These are small farinaceous berries, of a yellow colour and delicious taste, which I knew to be the fruit of the rhamnus lotus of Linnæus.

The lotus is very common in all the kingdoms which I visited; but is found in the greatest plenty on the sandy soil of Kaarta, Ludamar, and the northern parts of Bambarra, where it is one of the most common shrubs of the country.I had observed the same species at Gambia.

As this shrub is found in Tunis, and also in the negro kingdoms, and as it furnishes the natives of the latter with a food resembling bread, and also with a sweet liquor which is much relished by them, there can be little doubt of its being the lotus mentioned by Pliny as the food of the Libyan Lotophagi. An army may very well have been fed with the bread I have tasted, made of the meal of the fruit, as is said by Pliny to have been done in Libya; and as the taste of the bread is sweet and agreeable, it is not likely that the soldiers would complain of it.

We arrived in the evening at the village of Toorda; when all the rest of the king's people turned back except two, who remained with me as guides to Jarra.

February 15. - I departed from Toorda, and about two o'clock came to a considerable town, called Funingkedy. As we approached the town the inhabitants were much alarmed; for, as one of my guides wore a turban, they mistook us for some Moorish banditti. This misapprehension was soon cleared up, and we were well received by a Gambia slatee, who resides at this town, and at whose house we lodged.

February 16. - We were informed that a number of people would go from this town to Jarra on the day following; and as the road was much infested by the Moors we resolved to stay and accompany the travellers.

About two o'clock, as I was lying asleep upon a bullock's hide behind the door of the hut, I was awakened by the screams of women, and a general clamour and confusion among the inhabitants. At first I suspected that the Bambarrans had actually entered the town; but observing my boy upon the top of one of the huts, I called to him to know what was the matter. He informed me that the Moors were come a second time to steal the cattle, and that they were now close to the town. I mounted the roof of the hut, and observed a large herd of bullocks coming towards the town, followed by five Moors on horseback, who drove the cattle forward with their muskets. When they had reached the wells which are close to the town, the Moors selected from the herd sixteen of the finest beasts, and drove them off at full cell gallop. During this transaction the townspeople, to the number of five hundred, stood collected close to the walls of the town; and when the Moors drove the cattle away, though they passed within pistol-shot of them, the inhabitants scarcely made a show of resistance. I only saw four muskets fired, which, being loaded with gunpowder of the negroes' own manufacture, did no execution. Shortly after this I observed a number of people supporting a young man on horseback, and conducting him slowly towards the town. This was one of the herdsmen, who, attempting to throw his spear, had been wounded by a shot from one of the Moors. His mother walked on before, quite frantic with grief, clapping her hands, and enumerating the good qualities of her son. "Ee maffo fenio!" ("He never told a lie!") said the disconsolate mother as her wounded son was carried in at the gate - "Ee maffo fonio abada!" ("He never told a lie; no, never!") When they had conveyed him to his hut, and laid him upon a mat, all the spectators joined in lamenting his fate, by screaming and howling in the most piteous manner.

After their grief had subsided a little, I was desired to examine the wound. I found that the ball had passed quite through his leg, having fractured both bones a little below the knee: the poor boy was faint from the loss of blood, and his situation withal so very precarious, that I could not console his relations with any great hopes of his recovery. However, to give him a possible chance, I observed to them that it was necessary to cut off his leg above the knee. This proposal made every one start with horror; they had never heard of such a method of cure, and would by no means give their consent to it; indeed, they evidently considered me a sort of cannibal for proposing so cruel and unheard-of an operation, which, in their opinion, would be attended with more pain and danger than the wound itself. The patient was therefore committed to the care of some old bashreens, who endeavoured to secure him a passage into paradise by whispering in his ear some Arabic sentences, and desiring him to repeat them. After many unsuccessful attempts, the poor heathen at last pronounced, "La illah el Allah, Mahamet rasowl allahi" ("There is but one God, and Mohammed is his Prophet"); and the disciples of the Prophet assured his mother that her son had given sufficient evidence of his faith, and would be happy in a future state. He died the same evening.

February 17. - My guides informed me that in order to avoid the Moorish banditti it was necessary to travel in the night; we accordingly departed from Funingkedy in the afternoon, accompanied by about thirty people, carrying their effects with them into Ludamar, for fear of the war. We travelled with great silence and expedition until midnight, when we stopped in a sort of enclosure, near a small village; but the thermometer being so low as 68 degrees, none of the negroes could sleep on account of the cold.

At daybreak on the 18th we resumed our journey, and at eight o'clock passed Simbing, the frontier village of Ludamar, situated on a narrow pass between two rocky hills, and surrounded with a high wall. From this village Major Houghton (being deserted by his negro servants, who refused to follow him into the Moorish country) wrote his last letter with a pencil to Dr. Laidley. This brave but unfortunate man, heaving surmounted many difficulties, had taken a northerly direction, had endeavoured to pass through the kingdom of Ludamar, where I afterwards learned the following particulars concerning his melancholy fate:- On his arrival at Jarra he got acquainted with certain Moorish merchants who were travelling to Tisheet (a place near the salt pits in the Great Desert, ten days' journey to the northward) to purchase salt; and the Major, at the expense of a musket and some tobacco, engaged them to convey him thither. It is impossible to form any other opinion on this determination than that the Moors intentionally deceived him, either with regard to the route that he wished to pursue, or the state of the intermediate country between Jarra and Timbuctoo. Their intention probably was to rob and leave him in the desert. At the end of two days he suspected their treachery, and insisted on returning to Jarra. Finding him persist in this determination, the Moors robbed him of everything he possessed, and went off with their camels; the poor Major being thus deserted, returned on foot to a watering-place in possession of the Moors, called Tarra. He had been some days without food, and the unfeeling Moors refusing to give him any, he sank at last under his distresses. Whether he actually perished of hunger, or was murdered outright by the savage Mohammedans, is not certainly known; his body was dragged into the woods, and I was shown at a distance the spot where his remains were left to perish.

About four miles to the north of Simbing we came to a small stream of water, where we observed a number of wild horses they were all of one colour, and galloped away from us at an easy rate, frequently stopping and looking back. The negroes hunt them for food, and their flesh is much esteemed.

About noon we arrived at Jarra, a large town situated at the bottom of some rocky hills.

CHAPTER IX

The town of Jarra is of considerable extent; the houses are built of clay and stone intermixed - the clay answering the purpose of mortar. It is situated in the Moorish kingdom of Ludamar; but the major part of the inhabitants are negroes, from the borders of the southern states, who prefer a precarious protection under the Moors, which they purchase by a tribute, rather than continue exposed to their predatory hostilities. The tribute they pay is considerable; and they manifest towards their Moorish superiors the most unlimited obedience and submission, and are treated by them with the utmost indignity and contempt. The Moors of this and the other states adjoining the country of the negroes resemble in their persons the mulattoes of the West Indies to so great a degree as not easily to be distinguished from them; and, in truth, the present generation seem to be a mixed race between the Moors (properly so called) of the north and the negroes of the south, possessing many of the worst qualities of both nations.

Of the origin of these Moorish tribes, as distinguished from the inhabitants of Barbary, from whom they are divided by the Great Desert, nothing further seems to be known than what is related by John Leo, the African, whose account may be abridged as follows:-

Before the Arabian conquest, about the middle of the seventh century, all the inhabitants of Africa, whether they were descended from Numidians, Phœnicians, Carthaginians, Romans, Vandals, or Goths, were comprehended under the general name of Mauri, or Moors.All these nations were converted to the religion of Mohammed during the Arabian empire under the Kaliphs.About this time many of the Numidian tribes, who led a wandering life in the desert, and supported themselves upon the produce of their cattle, retired southward across the Great Desert to avoid the fury of the Arabians; and by one of those tribes, says Leo (that of Zanhaga), were discovered, and conquered, the negro nations on the Niger.By the Niger is here undoubtedly meant the river of Senegal, which in the Mandingo language is Bafing, or the Black River.

To what extent these people are now spread over the African continent it is difficult to ascertain.There is reason to believe that their dominion stretches from west to east, in a narrow line or belt, from the mouth of the Senegal (on the northern side of that river) to the confines of Abyssinia.They are a subtle and treacherous race of people, and take every opportunity of cheating and plundering the credulous and unsuspecting negroes.But their manners and general habits of life will be best explained as incidents occur in the course of my narrative.

The difficulties we had already encountered, the unsettled state of the country, and, above all, the savage and overbearing deportment of the Moors, had so completely frightened my attendants that they declared they would rather relinquish every claim to reward than proceed one step farther to the eastward.Indeed, the danger they incurred of being seized by the Moors, and sold into slavery, became every day more apparent; and I could not condemn their apprehensions.In this situation, deserted by my attendants, and reflecting that my retreat was cut off by the war behind me, and that a Moorish country of ten days' journey lay before me, I applied to Daman to obtain permission from Ali, the chief or sovereign of Ludamar, that I might pass through his country unmolested into Bambarra; and I hired one of Daman's slaves to accompany me thither, as soon as such permission should be obtained.A messenger was despatched to Ali, who at this time was encamped near Benowm; and as a present was necessary in order to insure success, I sent him five garments of cotton cloth, which I purchased of Daman for one of my fowling-pieces.Fourteen days elapsed in settling this affair; but on the evening of the 26th of February, one of Ali's slaves arrived with directions, as he pretended, to conduct me in safety as far as Goomba, and told me I was to pay him one garment of blue cotton cloth for his attendance.My faithful boy, observing that I was about to proceed without him, resolved to accompany me; and told me, that though he wished me to turn back, he never entertained any serious thoughts of deserting me, but had been advised to it by Johnson, with a view to induce me to turn immediately for Gambia.

February 27. - I delivered most of my papers to Johnson, to convey them to Gambia as soon as possible, reserving a duplicate for myself in case of accidents. I likewise left in Daman's possession a bundle of clothes, and other things that were not absolutely necessary, for I wished to diminish my baggage as much as possible, that the Moors might have fewer inducements to plunder us.

Things being thus adjusted, we departed from Jarra in the forenoon, and slept at Troomgoomba, a small walled village, inhabited by a mixture of negroes and Moors. On the day following (February 28th) we reached Quira; and on the 29th, after a toilsome journey over a sandy country, we came to Compe, a watering-place belonging to the Moors; from whence, on the morning following, we proceeded to Deena, a large town, and, like Jarra, built of stone and clay. The Moors are here in greater proportion to the negroes than at Jarra. They assembled round the hut of the negro where I lodged, and treated me with the greatest insolence; they hissed, shouted, and abused me; they even spat in my face, with a view to irritate me, and afford them a pretext for seizing my baggage. But finding such insults had not the desired effect, they had recourse to the final and decisive argument, that I was a Christian, and of course that my property was lawful plunder to the followers of Mohammed. They accordingly opened my bundles, and robbed me of everything they fancied. My attendants, finding that everybody could rob me with impunity, insisted on returning to Jarra.

The day following (March 2nd), I endeavoured, by all the means in my power, to prevail upon my people to go on, but they still continued obstinate; and having reason to fear some further insult from the fanatic Moors, I resolved to proceed alone. Accordingly, the next morning, about two o'clock, I departed from Deena. It was moonlight, but the roaring of the wild beasts made it necessary to proceed with caution.

When I had reached a piece of rising ground about half a mile from the town, I heard somebody halloo, and, looking back, saw my faithful boy running after me. He informed me that Ali's men had gone back to Benowm, and that Daman's negro was about to depart for Jarra; but he said he had no doubt, if I would stop a little, that he could persuade the latter to accompany us. I waited accordingly, and in about an hour the boy returned with the negro; and we continued travelling over a sandy country, covered chiefly with the Asclepias gigantea, until mid-day, when we came to a number of deserted huts; and seeing some appearances of water at a little distance, I sent the boy to fill a soofroo; but as he was examining the place for water, the roaring of a lion, that was probably on the same pursuit, induced the frightened boy to return in haste, and we submitted patiently to the disappointment. In the afternoon we reached a town inhabited chiefly by Foulahs, called Samaming-koos.

Next morning (March 4th), we set out for Sampaka, which place we reached about two o'clock. On the road we observed immense quantities of locusts; the trees were quite black with them.

Sampaka is a large town, and when the Moors and Bambarrans were at war was thrice attacked by the former; but they were driven off with great loss, though the king of Bambarra was afterwards obliged to give up this, and all the other towns as far as Goomba, in order to obtain a peace. Here I lodged at the house of a negro who practised the art of making gunpowder. He showed me a bag of nitre, very white, but the crystals were much smaller than common. They procure it in considerable quantities from the ponds, which are filled in the rainy season, and to which the cattle resort for coolness during the heat of the day. When the water is evaporated, a white efflorescence is observed on the mud, which the natives collect and purify in such a manner as to answer their purpose. The Moors supply them with sulphur from the Mediterranean; and the process is completed by pounding the different articles together in a wooden mortar. The grains are very unequal, and the sound of its explosion is by no means so sharp as that produced by European gunpowder.

March 5. - We departed from Sampaka at daylight. About noon we stopped a little at a village called Dangali, and in the evening arrived at Dalli. We saw upon the road two large herds of camels feeding. When the Moors turn their camels to feed they tie up one of their fore-legs to prevent their straying. This happened to be a feast-day at Dalli, and the people were dancing before the dooty's house. But when they were informed that a white man was come into the town they left off dancing and came to the place where I lodged, walking in regular order, two and two, with the music before them. They play upon a sort of flute; but instead of blowing into a hole in the side they blow obliquely over the end, which is half shut by a thin piece of wood; they govern the holes on the side with their fingers, and play some simple and very plaintive airs. They continued to dance and sing until midnight, during which time I was surrounded by so great a crowd as made it necessary for me to satisfy their curiosity by sitting still.

March 6. - We stopped here this morning because some of the townspeople, who were going for Goomba on the day following, wished to accompany us; but in order to avoid the crowd of people which usually assembled in the evening we went to a negro village to the east of Dalli, called Samee, where we were kindly received by the hospitable dooty, who on this occasion killed two fine sheep, and invited his friends to come and feast with him.

March 7. - Our landlord was so proud of the honour of entertaining a white man that he insisted on my staying with him and his friends until the cool of the evening, when he said he would conduct me to the next village. As I was now within two days' journey of Goomba, I had no apprehensions from the Moors, and readily accepted the invitation. I spent the forenoon very pleasantly with these poor negroes; their company was the more acceptable, as the gentleness of their manners presented a striking contrast to the rudeness and barbarity of the Moors. They enlivened their conversation by drinking a fermented liquor made from corn - the same sort of beer that I have described in a former chapter; and better I never tasted in Great Britain.

In the midst of this harmless festivity, I flattered myself that all danger from the Moors was over. Fancy had already placed me on the banks of the Niger, and presented to my imagination a thousand delightful scenes in my future progress, when a party of Moors unexpectedly entered the hut, and dispelled the golden dream. They came, they said, by Ali's orders, to convey me to his camp at Benowm. If I went peaceably, they told me, I had nothing to fear; but if I refused they had orders to bring me by force. I was struck dumb by surprise and terror, which the Moors observing endeavoured to calm my apprehensions by repeating the assurance that I had nothing to fear. Their visit, they added, was occasioned by the curiosity of Ali's wife Fatima, who had heard so much about Christians that she was very anxious to see one: as soon as her curiosity should be satisfied, they had no doubt, they said, that Ali would give me a handsome present, and send a person to conduct me to Bambarra. Finding entreaty and resistance equally fruitless, I prepared to follow the messengers, and took leave of my landlord and his company with great reluctance. Accompanied by my faithful boy (for Daman's slave made his escape on seeing the Moors), we reached Dalli in the evening, where we were strictly watched by the Moors during the night.

March 8. - We were conducted by a circuitous path through the woods to Dangali, where we slept.

March 9. - We continued our journey, and in the afternoon arrived at Sampaka.

Next morning (March 10th) we set out for Samaming-koos. On the road we overtook a woman and two boys with an ass; she informed us that she was going for Bambarra, but had been stopped on the road by a party of Moors, who had taken most of her clothes and some gold from her; and that she would be under the necessity of returning to Deena till the fast moon was over. The same even the new moon was seen which ushered in the month Ramadan. Large fires were made in different parts of the town, and a greater quantity of victuals than usual dressed upon the occasion.

March 11. - By daylight the Moors were in readiness; but as I had suffered much from thirst on the road I made my boy fill a soofroo of water for my own use, for the Moors assured me that they should not taste either meat or drink until sunset. However, I found that the excessive heat of the sun, and the dust we raised in travelling, overcame their scruples, and made my soofroo a very useful part of our baggage. On our arrival at Deena, I went to pay my respects to one of Ali's sons. I found him sitting in a low hut, with five or six more of his companions, washing their hands and feet, and frequently taking water into their mouths, gargling and spitting it out again. I was no sooner seated than he handed me a double-barrelled gun, and told me to dye the stock of a blue colour, and repair one of the locks. I found great difficulty in persuading him that I knew nothing about the matter. "However," says he, "if you cannot repair the gun, you shall give me some knives and scissors immediately;" and when my boy, who acted as interpreter, assured him that I had no such articles, he hastily snatched up a musket that stood by him, cocked it, and putting the muzzle close to the boy's ear, would certainly have shot him dead upon the spot had not the Moors wrested the musket from him, and made signs for us to retreat.

March 12. - We departed from Deena towards Benowm, and about nine o'clock came to a korree, whence the Moors were preparing to depart to the southward, on account of the scarcity of water; here we filled our soofroo, and continued our journey over a hot sandy country, covered with small stunted shrubs, until about one o'clock, when the heat of the sun obliged us to stop. But our water being expended, we could not prudently remain longer than a few minutes to collect a little gum, which is an excellent succedaneum for water, as it keeps the mouth moist, and allays for a time the pain in the throat.

About five o'clock we came in sight of Benowm, the residence of Ali. It presented to the eye a great number of dirty-looking tents, scattered without order over a large space of ground; and among the tents appeared large herds of camels, cattle, and goats. We reached the skirts of this camp a little before sunset, and, with much entreaty, procured a little water. My arrival was no sooner observed than the people who drew water at the wells threw down their buckets; those in the tents mounted their horses, and men, women, and children, came running or galloping towards me. I soon found myself surrounded by such a crowd that I could scarcely move; one pulled my clothes, another took off my hat, a third stopped me to examine my waistcoat-buttons, and a fourth called out, "La illah el Allah, Mahamet rasowl allahi" - ("There is but one God, and Mohammed is his Prophet") - and signified, in a threatening manner, that I must repeat those words. We reached at length the king's tent, where we found a great number of people, men and women, assembled. Ali was sitting upon a black leather cushion, clipping a few hairs from his upper lip, a female attendant holding up a looking-glass before him. He appeared to be an old man of the Arab cast, with a long white beard; and he had a sullen and indignant aspect. He surveyed me with attention, and inquired of the Moors if I could speak Arabic. Being answered in the negative, he appeared much surprised, and continued silent. The surrounding attendants, and especially the ladies, were abundantly more inquisitive: they asked a thousand questions, inspected every part of my apparel, searched my pockets, and obliged me to unbutton my waistcoat, and display the whiteness of my skin; they even counted my toes and fingers, as if they doubted whether I was in truth a human being. In a little time the priest announced evening prayers; but before the people departed, the Moor who had acted as interpreter informed me that Ali was about to present me with something to eat; and looking round, I observed some boys bringing a wild hog, which they tied to one of the tent strings, and Ali made signs to me to kill and dress it for supper. Though I was very hungry, I did not think it prudent to eat any part of an animal so much detested by the Moors, and therefore told him that I never ate such food. They then untied the hog, in hopes that it would run immediately at me - for they believe that a great enmity subsists between hogs and Christians - but in this they were disappointed, for the animal no sooner regained his liberty than he began to attack indiscriminately every person that came in his way, and at last took shelter under the couch upon which the king was sitting. The assembly being thus dissolved, I was conducted to the tent of Ali's chief slave, but was not permitted to enter, nor allowed to touch anything belonging to it. I requested something to eat, and a little boiled corn, with salt and water, was at length sent me in a wooden bowl; and a mat was spread upon the sand before the tent, on which I passed the night, surrounded by the curious multitude.

At sunrise, Ali, with a few attendants, came on horseback to visit me, and signified that he had provided a hut for me, where I would be sheltered from the sun. I was accordingly conducted thither, and found the hut comparatively cool and pleasant.

I was no sooner seated in this my new habitation than the Moors assembled in crowds to behold me; but I found it rather a troublesome levée, for I was obliged to take off one of my stockings, and show them my foot, and even to take off my jacket and waistcoat, to show them how my clothes were put on and off; they were much delighted with the curious contrivance of buttons. All this was to be repeated to every succeeding visitor; for such as had already seen these wonders insisted on their friends seeing the same; and in this manner I was employed, dressing and undressing, buttoning and unbuttoning, from noon till night. About eight o'clock, Ali sent me for supper some kouskous and salt and water, which was very acceptable, being the only victuals I had tasted since morning.

I observed that in the night the Moors kept regular watch, and frequently looked into the hut to see if I was asleep; and if it was quite dark, they would light a wisp of grass. About two o'clock in the morning a Moor entered the hut, probably with a view to steal something, or perhaps to murder me; and groping about he laid his hand upon my shoulder. As night visitors were at best but suspicious characters, I sprang up the moment he laid his hand upon me; and the Moor, in his haste to get off, stumbled over my boy, and fell with his face upon the wild hog, which returned the attack by biting the Moor's arm. The screams of this man alarmed the people in the king's tent, who immediately conjectured that I had made my escape, and a number of them mounted their horses, and prepared to pursue me. I observed upon this occasion that Ali did not sleep in his own tent, but came galloping upon a white horse from a small tent at a considerable distance; indeed, the tyrannical and cruel behaviour of this man made him so jealous of every person around him that even his own slaves and domestics knew not where he slept. When the Moors had explained to him the cause of this outcry they all went away, and I was permitted to sleep quietly until morning.

March 13. - With the returning day commenced the same round of insult and irritation - the boys assembled to beat the hog, and the men and women to plague the Christian. It is impossible for me to describe the behaviour of a people who study mischief as a science, and exult in the miseries and misfortunes of their fellow-creatures.

CHAPTER X

The Moors, though very indolent themselves, are rigid task-masters, and keep every person under them in full employment. My boy Demba was sent to the woods to collect withered grass for Ali's horses; and after a variety of projects concerning myself, they at last found out an employment for me: this was no other than the respectable office of barber. I was to make my first exhibition in this capacity in the royal presence, and to be honoured with the task of shaving the head of the young prince of Ludamar. I accordingly seated myself upon the sand, and the boy, with some hesitation, sat down beside me. A small razor, about three inclines long, was put into my hand, and I was ordered to proceed; but whether from my own want of skill, or the improper shape of the instrument, I unfortunately made a slight incision in the boy's head at the very commencement of the operation; and the king, observing the awkward manner in which I held the razor, concluded that his son's head was in very improper hands, and ordered me to resign the razor and walk out of the tent. This I considered as a very fortunate circumstance; for I had laid it down as a rule to make myself as useless and insignificant as possible, as the only means of recovering my liberty.

March 18. - Four Moors arrived from Jarra with Johnson my interpreter, having seized him before he had received any intimation of my confinement, and bringing with them a bundle of clothes that I had left at Daman Jumma's house, for my use in case I should return by the way of Jarra. Johnson was led into Ali's tent and examined; the bundle was opened, and I was sent for to explain the use of the different articles. I was happy, however, to find that Johnson had committed my papers to the charge of one of Daman's wives. When I had satisfied Ali's curiosity respecting the different articles of apparel the bundle was again tied up, and put into a large cow-skin bag that stood in a corner of the tent. The same evening Ali sent three of his people to inform me that there were many thieves in the neighbourhood, and that to prevent the rest of my things from being stolen it was necessary to convey them all into his tent. My clothes, instruments, and everything that belonged to me, were accordingly carried away; and though the heat and dust made clean linen very necessary and refreshing, I could not procure a single shirt out of the small stock I had brought along with me. Ali was, however, disappointed by not finding among my effects the quantity of gold and amber that he expected; but to make sure of everything he sent the same people, on the morning following, to examine whether I had anything concealed about my person. They, with their usual rudeness, searched every part of my apparel, and stripped me of all my gold, amber, my watch, and one of my pocket-compasses; I had, fortunately, in the night, buried the other compass in the sand - and this, with the clothes I had on, was all that the tyranny of Ali had now left me.

The gold and amber were highly gratifying to Moorish avarice, but the pocket-compass soon became an object of superstitious curiosity. Ali was very desirous to be informed why that small piece of iron, the needle, always pointed to the Great Desert; and I found myself somewhat puzzled to answer the question. To have pleaded my ignorance would have created a suspicion that I wished to conceal the real truth from him; I therefore told him that my mother resided far beyond the sands of Sahara, and that whilst she was alive the piece of iron would always point that way, and serve as a guide to conduct me to her, and that if she was dead it would point to her grave. Ali now looked at the compass with redoubled amazement; turned it round and round repeatedly; but observing that it always pointed the same way, he took it up with great caution and returned it to me, manifesting that he thought there was something of magic in it, and that he was afraid of keeping so dangerous an instrument in his possession.

March 20. - This morning a council of chief men was held in Ali's tent respecting me. Their decisions, though they were all unfavourable to me, were differently related by different persons. Some said that they intended to put me to death; others that I was only to lose my right hand; but the most probable account was that which I received from Ali's own son, a boy about nine years of age, who came to me in the evening, and, with much concern, informed me that his uncle had persuaded his father to put out my eyes, which they said resembled those of a cat, and that all the bushreens had approved of this measure. His father, however, he said, would not put the sentence into execution until Fatima, the queen, who was at present in the north, had seen me.

March 21. - Anxious to know my destiny, I went to the king early in the morning; and as a number of bushreens were assembled, I thought this a favourable opportunity of discovering their intentions. I therefore began by begging his permission to return to Jarra, which was flatly refused. His wife, he said, had not yet seen me, and I must stay until she came to Benowm, after which I should be at liberty to depart; and that my horse, which had been taken away from me the day after I arrived, should be again restored to me. Unsatisfactory as this answer was, I was forced to appear pleased; and as there was little hope of making my escape at this season of the year, on account of the excessive heat, and the total want of water in the woods, I resolved to wait patiently until the rains had set in, or until some more favourable opportunity should present itself. But "hope deferred maketh the heart sick." This tedious procrastination from day to day, and the thoughts of travelling through the negro kingdoms in the rainy season, which was now fast approaching, made me very melancholy; and having passed a restless night, I found myself attacked in the morning by a smart fever. I had wrapped myself close up in my cloak with a view to induce perspiration, and was asleep, when a party of Moors entered the hut, and with their usual rudeness pulled the cloak from me. I made signs to them that I was sick, and wished much to sleep, but I solicited in vain; my distress was matter of sport to them, and they endeavoured to heighten it by every means in their power. In this perplexity I left my hut, and walked to some shady trees at a little distance from the camp, where I lay down. But even here persecution followed me, and solitude was thought too great an indulgence for a distressed Christian. Ali's son, with a number of horsemen, came galloping to the place, and ordered me to rise and follow them. I begged they would allow me to remain where I was, if it was only for a few hours; but they paid little attention to what I said, and, after a few threatening words, one of them pulled out a pistol from a leather bag that was fastened to the pommel of his saddle, and presenting it towards me, snapped it twice. He did this with so much indifference, that I really doubted whether the pistol was loaded. He cocked it a third time, and was striking the flint with a piece of steel, when I begged them to desist, and returned with them to the camp. When we entered Ali's tent we found him much out of humour. He called for the Moor's pistol, and amused himself for some time with opening and shutting the pan; at length taking up his powder-horn, he fresh primed it, and, turning round to me with a menacing look, said something in Arabic which I did not understand. I desired my boy, who was sitting before the tent, to inquire what offence I had committed; when I was informed, that having gone out of the camp without Ali's permission, they suspected that I had some design of making my escape; and that, in future, if I was seen without the skirts of the camp, orders had been given that I should be shot by the first person that observed me.

In the afternoon the horizon to the eastward was thick and hazy, and the

Moors prognosticated a sand wind, which accordingly commenced on the morning following, and lasted, with slight intermissions, for two days. The force of the wind was not in itself very great; it was what a seaman would have denominated a stiff breeze; but the quantity of sand and dust carried before it was such as to darken the whole atmosphere.

About this time all the women of the camp had their feet and the ends of their fingers stained of a dark saffron colour. I could never ascertain whether this was done from motives of religion, or by way of ornament.

March 28. - This morning a large herd of cattle arrived from the eastward, and one of the drivers, to whom Ali had lent my horse, came into my hut with the leg of an antelope as a present, and told me that my horse was standing before Ali's tent. In a little time Ali sent one of his slaves to inform me that in the afternoon I must be in readiness to ride out with him, as he intended to show me to some of his women.

About four o'clock, Ali, with six of his courtiers, came riding to my hut, and told me to follow them. I readily complied. But here a new difficulty occurred. The Moors, accustomed to a loose and easy dress, could not reconcile themselves to the appearance of my nankeen breeches, which they said were not only inelegant, but, on account of their tightness, very indecent; and as this was a visit to ladies, Ali ordered my boy to bring out the loose cloak which I had always worn since my arrival at Benowm, and told me to wrap it close round me. We visited the tents of four different ladies, at every one of which I was presented with a bowl of milk and water. All these ladies were remarkably corpulent, which is considered here as the highest mark of beauty. They were very inquisitive, and examined my hair and skin with great attention, but affected to consider me as a sort of inferior being to themselves, and would knit their brows, and seem to shudder when they looked at the whiteness of my skin.

The Moors are certainly very good horsemen. They ride without fear - their saddles being high before and behind, afford them a very secure seat; and if they chance to fall, the whole country is so soft and sandy that they are very seldom hurt. Their greatest pride, and one of their principal amusements, is to put the horse to its full speed, and then stop him with a sudden jerk, so as frequently to bring him down upon his haunches. Ali always rode upon a milk-white horse, with its tail dyed red. He never walked, unless when he went to say his prayers; and even in the night two or three horses were always kept ready saddled at a little distance from his own tent. The Moors set a very high value upon their horses; for it is by their superior fleetness that they are enabled to make so many predatory excursions into the negro countries. They feed them three or four times a day, and generally give them a large quantity of sweet milk in the evening, which the horses appear to relish very much.

April 3. - This forenoon, a child, which had been some time sickly, died in the next tent; and the mother and relations immediately began the death-howl. They were joined by a number of female visitors, who came on purpose to assist at this melancholy concert. I had no opportunity of seeing the burial, which is generally performed secretly, in the dusk of the evening, and frequently at only a few yards' distance from the tent. Over the grave they plant one particular shrub, and no stranger is allowed to pluck a leaf, or even to touch it - so great a veneration have they for the dead.

April 7. - About four o'clock in the afternoon a whirlwind passed through the camp with such violence that it overturned three tents, and blew down one side of my hut. These whirlwinds come from the Great Desert, and at this season of the year are so common that I have seen five or six of them at one time. They carry up quantities of sand to an amazing height, which resemble, at a distance, so many moving pillars of smoke.

The scorching heat of the sun, upon a dry and sandy country, makes the air insufferably hot. Ali having robbed me of my thermometer, I had no means of forming a comparative judgment; but in the middle of the day, when the beams of the vertical sun are seconded by the scorching wind from the desert, the ground is frequently heated to such a degree as not to be borne by the naked foot. Even the negro slaves will not run from one tent to another without their sandals. At this time of the day the Moors lie stretched at length in their tents, either asleep, or unwilling to move; and I have often felt the wind so hot, that I could not hold my hand in the current of air which came through the crevices of my hut without feeling sensible pain.

April 8. - This day the wind blew from the south-west; and in the night there was a heavy shower of rain, accompanied with thunder and lightning.

April 10. - In the evening the tabala, or large drum, was beat to announce a wedding, which was held at one of the neighbouring tents. A great number of people of both sexes assembled, but without that mirth and hilarity which take place at a negro wedding. Here was neither singing nor dancing, nor any other amusement that I could perceive. A woman was beating the drum, and the other women joining at times like a chorus, by setting up a shrill scream, and at the same time moving their tongues from one side of the mouth to the other with great celerity. I was soon tired, and had returned into my hut, where I was sitting almost asleep, when an old woman entered with a wooden bowl in her hand, and signified that she had brought me a present from the bride. Before I could recover from the surprise which this message created, the woman discharged tine contents of the bowl full in my face. Finding that it was the same sort of holy water with which, among the Hottentots, a priest is said to sprinkle a newly-married couple, I began to suspect that the old lady was actuated by mischief or malice; but she gave me seriously to understand that it was a nuptial benediction from the bride's own person, and which, on such occasions, is always received by the young unmarried Moors as a mark of distinguished favour. This being the case, I wiped my face, and sent my acknowledgments to the lady. The wedding drum continued to beat, and the women to sing, or rather whistle, all night. About nine in the morning the bride was brought in state from her mother's tent, attended by a number of women who carried her tent (a present from the husband), some bearing up the poles, others holding by the strings; and in this manner they marched, whistling as formerly, until they came to the place appointed for her residence, where they pitched the tent. The husband followed, with a number of men, leading four bullocks, which they tied to the tent strings; and having killed another, and distributed the beef among the people, the ceremony was concluded.

CHAPTER XI

One whole month had now elapsed since I was led into captivity, during which time each returning day brought me fresh distresses. I watched the lingering course of the sun with anxiety, and blessed his evening beams as they shined a yellow lustre along the sandy floor of my hut; for it was then that my oppressors left me, and allowed me to pass the sultry night in solitude and reflection.

About midnight a bowl of kouskous, with some salt and water, were brought for me and my two attendants. This was our common fare, and it was all that was allowed us to allay the cravings of hunger and support nature for the whole of the following day; for it is to be observed that this was the Mohammedan Lent, and as the Moors keep the fast with a religious strictness, they thought it proper to compel me, though a Christian, to similar observance. Time, however, somewhat reconciled me to my situation. I found that I could bear hunger and thirst better than I expected; and at length I endeavoured to beguile the tedious hours by learning to write Arabic.

April 14. - As Queen Fatima had not yet arrived, Ali proposed to go to the north and bring her back with him; but as the place was two days' journey from Benowm it was necessary to have some refreshment on the road; and Ali, suspicious of those about him, was so afraid of being poisoned, that he never ate anything but what was dressed under his own immediate inspection. A fine bullock was therefore killed, and the flesh being cut up into thin slices, was dried in the sun; and this, with two bags of dry kouskous, formed his travelling provisions.

Previous to his departure, the black people of the town of Benowm came, according to their annual custom, to show their arms, and bring their stipulated tribute of corn and cloth. They were but badly armed - twenty-two with muskets, forty or fifty with bows and arrows, and nearly the same number of men and boys with spears only. They arranged themselves before the tent, where they waited until their arms were examined, and some little disputes settled.

About midnight on the 16th, Ali departed quietly from Benowm, accompanied by a few attendants. He was expected to return in the course of nine or ten days.

April 18. - Two days after the departure of Ali a shereef arrived with salt and some other articles from Walet, the capital of the kingdom of Biroo. As there was no tent appropriated for him, he took up his abode in the same hut with me. He seemed to be a well-informed man, and his acquaintance both with the Arabic and Bambarra tongues enabled him to travel with ease and safety through a number of kingdoms; for though his place of residence was Walet, he had visited Houssa, and had lived some years at Timbuctoo. Upon my inquiring so particularly about the distance from Walet to Timbuctoo, he asked me if I intended to travel that way; and being answered in the affirmative, he shook his head, and said it would not do; for that Christians were looked upon there as the devil's children, and enemies to the Prophet. From him I learned the following particulars:- That Houssa was the largest town he had ever seen: that Walet was larger than Timbuctoo, but being remote from the Niger, and its trade consisting chiefly of salt, it was not so much resorted to by strangers: that between Benowm and Walet was ten days' journey; but the road did not lead through any remarkable towns, and travellers supported themselves by purchasing milk from the Arabs, who keep their herds by the watering-places: two of the days' journeys was over a sandy country, without water. From Walet to Timbuctoo was eleven days more; but water was more plentiful, and the journey was usually performed upon bullocks. He said there were many Jews at Timbuctoo, but they all spoke Arabic, and used the same prayers as the Moors. He frequently pointed his hand to the south-east quarter, or rather the east by south, observing that Timbuctoo was situated in that direction; and though I made him repeat this information again and again, I never found him to vary more than half a point, which was to the southward.

April 24. - This morning Shereef Sidi Mahomed Moora Abdalla, a native of Morocco, arrived with five bullocks loaded with salt. He had formerly resided some months at Gibraltar, where he had picked up as much English as enabled him to make himself understood. He informed me that he had been five months in coming from Santa Cruz; but that great part of the time had been spent in trading. When I requested him to enumerate the days employed in travelling from Morocco to Benowm, he gave them as follows: To Swera, three days; to Agadier, three; to Jinikin, ten; to Wadenoon, four; to Lakeneig, five; to Zeeriwin-zerimani, five; to Tisheet, ten; to Benowm, ten - in all, fifty days: but travellers usually rest a long while at Jinikin and Tisheet - at the latter of which places they dig the rock salt, which is so great an article of commerce with the negroes.

In conversing with these shereefs, and the different strangers that resorted to the camp, I passed my time with rather less uneasiness than formerly. On the other hand, as the dressing of my victuals was now left entirely to the care of Ali's slaves, over whom I had not the smallest control, I found myself but ill supplied, worse even than in the fast month: for two successive nights they neglected to send us our accustomed meal; and though my boy went to a small negro town near the camp, and begged with great diligence from hut to hut, he could only procure a few handfuls of ground nuts, which he readily shared with me.

We had been for some days in daily expectation of Ali's return from Saheel (or the north country) with his wife Fatima. In the meanwhile, Mansong, king of Bambarra, as I have related in Chapter VIII., had sent to Ali for a party of horse to assist in storming Gedingooma. With this demand Ali had not only refused to comply, but had treated the messengers with great haughtiness and contempt; upon which Mansong gave up all thoughts of taking the town, and prepared to chastise Ali for his contumacy.

Things were in this situation when, on the 29th of April, a messenger arrived at Benowm with the disagreeable intelligence that the Bambarra army was approaching the frontiers of Ludamar. This threw the whole country into confusion, and in the afternoon Ali's son, with about twenty horsemen, arrived at Benowm. He ordered all the cattle to be driven away immediately, all the tents to be struck, and the people to hold themselves in readiness to depart at daylight the next morning.

April 30. - At daybreak the whole camp was in motion. The baggage was carried upon bullocks - the two tent poles being placed one on each side, and the different wooden articles of the tent distributed in like manner; the tent cloth was thrown over all, and upon this was commonly placed one or two women; for the Moorish women are very bad walkers. The king's favourite concubines rode upon camels, with a saddle of a particular construction, and a canopy to shelter them from the sun. We proceeded to the northward until noon, when the king's son ordered the whole company, except the tents, to enter a thick low wood which was upon our right. I was sent along with the two tents, and arrived in the evening at a negro town called Farani: here we pitched the tents in an open place at no great distance from the town.

May 1. - As I had some reason to suspect that this day was also to be considered as a fast, I went in the morning to the negro town of Farani, and begged some provisions from the dooty, who readily supplied my wants, and desired me to come to his house every day during my stay in the neighbourhood. - These hospitable people are looked upon by the Moors as an abject race of slaves, and are treated accordingly.

May 3. - We departed from the vicinity of Farani, and after a circuitous route through the woods, arrived at Ali's camp in the afternoon. This encampment was larger than that of Benowm, and was situated un the middle of a thick wood, about two miles distant from a negro town called Bubaker.I immediately waited upon Ali, in order to pay my respects to Queen Fatima, who had come with him from Saheel.He seemed much pleased with my coming, shook hands with me, and informed his wife that I was the Christian.She was a woman of the Arab caste, with long black hair, and remarkably corpulent.She appeared at first rather shocked at the thought of having a Christian so near her; but when I had, by means of a negro boy who spoke the Mandingo and Arabic tongues, answered a great many questions which her curiosity suggested respecting the country of the Christians, she seemed more at ease, and presented me with a bowl of milk, which I considered as a very favourable omen.

The heat was now almost insufferable - all nature seemed sinking under it.The distant country presented to the eye a dreary expanse of sand, with a few stunted trees and prickly bushes, in the shade of which the hungry cattle licked up the withered grass, while the camels and goats picked off the scanty foliage.The scarcity of water was greater here than at Benowm.Day and night the wells were crowded with cattle, lowing and fighting with each other to come at the troughs.Excessive thirst made many of them furious; others, being too weak to contend for the water, endeavoured to quench their thirst by devouring the black mud from the gutters near the wells, which they did with great avidity, though it was commonly fatal to them.

One night, having solicited in vain for water at the camp, and been quite feverish, I resolved to try my fortune at the wells, which were about half a mile distant from the camp.Accordingly I set out about midnight, and being guided by the lowing of the cattle, soon arrived at the place, where I found the Moors very busy drawing water.I requested permission to drink, but was driven away with outrageous abuse.Passing, however, from one well to another, I came at last to one where there was only an old man and two boys.I made the same request to this man, and he immediately drew me up a bucket of water; but, as I was about to take hold of it, he recollected that I was a Christian, and fearing that his bucket might be polluted by my lips, he dashed the water into the trough, and told me to drink from thence.Though this trough was none of the largest, and three cows were already drinking from it, I resolved to come in for my share; and kneeling down thrust my head between two of the cows, and drank with great pleasure until the water was nearly exhausted, and the cows began to contend with each other for the last mouthful.

In adventures of this nature I passed the sultry month of May, during which no material change took place in my situation.Ali still considered me as a lawful prisoner; and Fatima, though she allowed me a larger quantity of victuals than I had been accustomed to receive at Benowm, had as yet said nothing on the subject of my release. In the meantime, the frequent changes of the wind, the gathering clouds, and distant lightning, with other appearances of approaching rain, indicated that the wet season was at hand, when the Moors annually evacuate the country of the negroes, and return to the skirts of the Great Desert. This made me consider that my fate was drawing towards a crisis, and I resolved to wait for the event without any seeming uneasiness; but circumstances occurred which produced a change in my favour more suddenly than I had foreseen, or had reason to expect. The case was this:- The fugitive Kaartans, who had taken refuge in Ludamar, as I have related in Chapter VIII., finding that the Moors were about to leave them, and dreading the resentment of their own sovereign, whom they had so basely deserted, offered to treat with Ali for two hundred Moorish horsemen, to co-operate with them in an effort to expel Daisy from Gedingooma; for until Daisy should be vanquished or humbled they considered that they could neither return to their native towns nor live in security in any of the neighbouring kingdoms. With a view to extort money from these people by means of this treaty, Ali despatched his son to Jarra, and prepared to follow him in the course of a few days. This was an opportunity of too great consequence to me to be neglected. I immediately applied to Fatima, who, I found, had the chief direction in all affairs of state, and begged her interest with Ali to give me permission to accompany him to Jarra. This request, after some hesitation, was favourably received. Fatima looked kindly on me, and, I believe, was at length moved with compassion towards me. My bundles were brought from the large cow-skin bag that stood in the corner of Ali's tent, and I was ordered to explain the use of the different articles, and show the method of putting on the boots, stockings, andc. - with all which I cheerfully complied, and was told that in the course of a few days I should be at liberty to depart.

Believing, therefore, that I should certainly find the means of escaping from Jarra, if I should once get thither, I now freely indulged the pleasing hope that my captivity would soon terminate; and happily not having been disappointed in this idea, I shall pause in this place to collect and bring into one point of view such observations on the Moorish character and country as I had no fair opportunity of introducing into the preceding narrative.

CHAPTER XII

The Moors of this part of Africa are divided into many separate tribes, of which the most formidable, according to what was reported to me, are those of Trasart and Il Braken, which inhabit the northern bank of the Senegal river. The tribes of Gedumah, Jaffnoo, and Ludamar, though not so numerous as the former, are nevertheless very powerful and warlike, and are each governed by a chief, or king, who exercises absolute jurisdiction over his own horde, without acknowledging allegiance to a common sovereign. In time of peace the employment of the people is pasturage. The Moors, indeed, subsist chiefly on the flesh of their cattle, and are always in the extreme of either gluttony or abstinence. In consequence of the frequent and severe fasts which their religion enjoins, and the toilsome journeys which they sometimes undertake across the desert, they are enabled to bear both hunger and thirst with surprising fortitude; but whenever opportunities occur of satisfying their appetite they generally devour more at one meal than would serve a European for three. They pay but little attention to agriculture, purchasing their corn, cotton, cloth, and other necessaries from the negroes, in exchange for salt, which they dig from the pits in the Great Desert.

The natural barrenness of the country is such that it furnishes but few materials for manufacture. The Moors, however, contrive to weave a strong cloth, with which they cover their tents; the thread is spun by their women from the hair of goats, and they prepare the hides of their cattle so as to furnish saddles, bridles, pouches, and other articles of leather. They are likewise sufficiently skilful to convert the native iron, which they procure from the negroes, into spears and knives, and also into pots for boiling their food; but their sabres, and other weapons, as well as their firearms and ammunition, they purchase from the Europeans, in exchange for the negro slaves which they obtain in their predatory excursions. Their chief commerce of this kind is with the French traders on the Senegal river.

The Moors are rigid Mohammedans, and possess, with the bigotry and superstition, all the intolerance of their sect. They have no mosques at Benowm, but perform their devotions in a sort of open shed, or enclosure, made of mats. The priest is, at the same time, schoolmaster to the juniors. His pupils assemble every evening before his tent; where, by the light of a large fire, made of brushwood and cow's dung, they are taught a few sentences from the Koran, and are initiated into the principles of their creed. Their alphabet differs but little from that in Richardson's Arabic Grammar. They always write with the vowel points. Their priests even affect to know something of foreign literature. The priest of Benowm assured me that he could read the writings of the Christians: he showed me a number of barbarous characters, which he asserted were the Roman alphabet; and he produced another specimen, equally unintelligible, which he declared to be the Kallam il Indi, or Persian. His library consisted of nine volumes in quarto; most of them, I believe, were books of religion - for the name of Mohammed appeared in red letters in almost every page of each. His scholars wrote their lessons upon thin boards, paper being too expensive for general use. The boys were diligent enough, and appeared to possess a considerable share of emulation - carrying their boards slung over their shoulders when about their common employments. When a boy has committed to memory a few of their prayers, and can read and write certain parts of the Koran, he is reckoned sufficiently instructed; and with this slender stock of learning commences his career of life. Proud of his acquirements, he surveys with contempt the unlettered negro; and embraces every opportunity of displaying his superiority over such of his countrymen as are not distinguished by the same accomplishments.

The education of the girls is neglected altogether: mental accomplishments are but little attended to by the women; nor is the want of them considered by the men as a defect in the female character. They are regarded, I believe, as an inferior species of animals; and seem to be brought up for no other purpose than that of administering to the sensual pleasures of their imperious masters. Voluptuousness is therefore considered as their chief accomplishment, and slavish submission as their indispensable duty.

The Moors have singular ideas of feminine perfection. The gracefulness of figure and motion, and a countenance enlivened by expression, are by no means essential points in their standard. With them corpulence and beauty appear to be terms nearly synonymous. A woman of even moderate pretensions must be one who cannot walk without a slave under each arm to support her; and a perfect beauty is a load for a camel. In consequence of this prevalent taste for unwieldiness of bulk, the Moorish ladies take great pains to acquire it early in life; and for this purpose many of the young girls are compelled by their mothers to devour a great quantity of kouskous, and drink a large bowl of camel's milk every morning. It is of no importance whether the girl has an appetite or not; the kouskous and milk must be swallowed, and obedience is frequently enforced by blows. I have seen a poor girl sit crying, with the bowl at her lips, for more than an hour, and her mother, with a stick in her hand, watching her all the while, and using the stick without mercy whenever she observed that her daughter was not swallowing. This singular practice, instead of producing indigestion and disease, soon covers the young lady with that degree of plumpness which, in the eye of a Moor, is perfection itself.

As the Moors purchase all their clothing from the negroes, the women are forced to be very economical in the article of dress. In general they content themselves with a broad piece of cotton cloth, which is wrapped round the middle, and hangs down like a petticoat almost to the ground. To the upper part of this are sewed two square pieces, one before, and the other behind, which are fastened together over the shoulders. The head-dress is commonly a bandage of cotton cloth, with some parts of it broader than others, which serve to conceal the face when they walk in the sun. Frequently, however, when they go abroad, they veil themselves from head to foot.

The employment of the women varies according to their degrees of opulence.Queen Fatima, and a few others of high rank, like the great ladies in some parts of Europe, pass their time chiefly in conversing with their visitors, performing their devotions, or admiring their charms in a looking-glass.The women of inferior class employ themselves in different domestic duties.They are very vain and talkative; and when anything puts them out of humour they commonly vent their anger upon their female slaves, over whom they rule with severe and despotic authority, which leads me to observe that the condition of these poor captives is deplorably wretched.At daybreak they are compelled to fetch water from the wells in large skins, called girbas; and as soon as they have brought water enough to serve the family for the day, as well as the horses (for the Moors seldom give their horses the trouble of going to the wells), they are then employed in pounding the corn and dressing the victuals.This being always done in the open air, the slaves are exposed to the combined heat of the sun, the sand, and the fire.In the intervals it is their business to sweep the tent, churn the milk, and perform other domestic offices.With all this they are badly fed, and oftentimes cruelly punished.

The men's dress, among the Moors of Ludamar, differs but little from that of the negroes, which has been already described, except that they have all adopted that characteristic of the Mohammedan sect, the turban, which is here universally made of white cotton cloth.Such of the Moors as have long beards display them with a mixture of pride and satisfaction, as denoting an Arab ancestry.Of this number was Ali himself; but among the generality of the people the hair is short and busy, and universally black.And here I may be permitted to observe, that if any one circumstance excited among them favourable thoughts towards my own person, it was my beard, which was now grown to an enormous length, and was always beheld with approbation or envy.I believe, in my conscience, they thought it too good a beard for a Christian.

The only diseases which I observed to prevail among the Moors were the intermittent fever and dysentery - for the cure of which nostrums are sometimes administered by their old women, but in general nature is left to her own operations.Mention was made to me of the small-pox as being sometimes very destructive; but it had not, to my knowledge, made its appearance in Ludamar while I was in captivity.That it prevails, however, among some tribes of the Moors, and that it is frequently conveyed by them to the negroes in the southern states, I was assured on the authority of Dr. Laidley, who also informed me that the negroes on the Gambia practise inoculation.

The administration of criminal justice, as far as I had opportunities of observing, was prompt and decisive: for although civil rights were but little regarded in Ludamar, it was necessary when crimes were committed that examples should sometimes be made.On such occasions the offender was brought before Ali, who pronounced, of his sole authority, what judgment he thought proper. But I understood that capital punishment was seldom or never inflicted, except on the negroes.

Although the wealth of the Moors consists chiefly in their numerous herds of cattle, yet, as the pastoral life does not afford full employment, the majority of the people are perfectly idle, and spend the day in trifling conversation about their horses, or in laying schemes of depredation on the negro villages.

Of the number of Ali's Moorish subjects I had no means of forming a correct estimate. The military strength of Ludamar consists in cavalry. They are well mounted, and appear to be very expert in skirmishing and attacking by surprise. Every soldier furnishes his own horse, and finds his accoutrements, consisting of a large sabre, a double-barrelled gun, a small red leather bag for holding his balls, and a powder bag slung over the shoulder. He has no pay, nor any remuneration but what arises from plunder. This body is not very numerous; for when Ali made war upon Bambarra I was informed that his whole force did not exceed two thousand cavalry. They constitute, however, by what I could learn, but a very small proportion of his Moorish subjects. The horses are very beautiful, and so highly esteemed that the negro princes will sometimes give from twelve to fourteen slaves for one horse.

Ludamar has for its northern boundary the great desert of Sahara. From the best inquiries I could make, this vast ocean of sand, which occupies so large a space in northern Africa, may be pronounced almost destitute of inhabitants, except where the scanty vegetation which appears in certain spots affords pasturage for the flocks of a few miserable Arabs, who wander from one well to another. In other places, where the supply of water and pasturage is more abundant, small parties of the Moors have taken up their residence. Here they live, in independent poverty, secure from the tyrannical government of Barbary. But the greater part of the desert, being totally destitute of water, is seldom visited by any human being, unless where the trading caravans trace out their toilsome and dangerous route across it. In some parts of this extensive waste the ground is covered with low stunted shrubs, which serve as landmarks for the caravans, and furnish the camels with a scanty forage. In other parts the disconsolate wanderer, wherever he turns, sees nothing around him but a vast interminable expanse of sand and sky - a gloomy and barren void, where the eye finds no particular object to rest upon, and the mind is filled with painful apprehensions of perishing with thirst.

The few wild animals which inhabit these melancholy regions are the antelope and the ostrich; their swiftness of foot enabling them to reach the distant watering-places. On the skirts of the desert, where water is more plentiful, are found lions, panthers, elephants, and wild bears.

Of domestic animals, the only one that can endure the fatigue of crossing the desert is the camel.By the particular conformation of the stomach he is enabled to carry a supply of water sufficient for ten or twelve days; his broad and yielding foot is well adapted for a sandy country; and, by a singular motion of his upper lip, he picks the smallest leaves from the thorny shrubs of the desert as he passes along.The camel is therefore the only beast of burden employed by the trading caravans which traverse the desert in different directions, from Barbary to Nigritia.As this useful and docile creature has been sufficiently described by systematical writers it is unnecessary for me to enlarge upon his properties.I shall only add that his flesh, though to my own taste dry and unsavoury, is preferred by the Moors to any other; and that the milk of the female is in universal esteem, and is indeed sweet, pleasant, and nutritive.

I have observed that the Moors, in their complexion, resemble the mulattoes of the West Indies; but they have something unpleasant in their aspect which the mulattoes have not.I fancied that I discovered in the features of most of them a disposition towards cruelty and low cunning; and I could never contemplate their physiognomy without feeling sensible uneasiness.From the staring wildness of their eyes a stranger would immediately set them down as a nation of lunatics.The treachery and malevolence of their character are manifest in their plundering excursions against the negro villages.Oftentimes without the smallest provocation, and sometimes under the fairest professions of friendship, they will suddenly seize upon the negroes' cattle, and even on the inhabitants themselves.The negroes very seldom retaliate.

Like the roving Arabs, the Moors frequently remove from one place to another, according to the season of the year or the convenience of pasturage.In the month of February, when the heat of the sun scorches up every sort of vegetation in the desert, they strike their tents and approach the negro country to the south, where they reside until the rains commence, in the month of July.At this time, having purchased corn and other necessaries from the negroes, in exchange for salt, they again depart to the northward, and continue in the desert until the rains are over, and that part of the country becomes burnt up and barren.

This wandering and restless way of life, while it inures them to hardships, strengthens at the same time the bonds of their little society, and creates in them an aversion towards strangers which is almost insurmountable.Cut off from all intercourse with civilised nations, and boasting an advantage over the negroes, by possessing, though in a very limited degree, the knowledge of letters, they are at once the vainest and proudest, and perhaps the most bigoted, ferocious, and intolerant of all the nations on the earth - combining in their character the blind superstition of the negro with the savage cruelty and treachery of the Arab.

CHAPTER XIII

Having, as hath been related, obtained permission to accompany Ali to Jarra, I took leave of Queen Fatima, who, with much grace and civility, returned me part of my apparel; and the evening before my departure, my horse, with the saddle and bridle, were sent me by Ali's order.

Early on the morning of the 26th of May I departed from the camp of Bubaker, accompanied by my two attendants, Johnson and Demba, and a number of Moors on horseback, Ali, with about fifty horsemen, having gone privately from the camp during the night. We stopped about noon at Farani, and were there joined by twelve Moors riding upon camels, and with them we proceeded to a watering-place in the woods, where we overtook Ali and his fifty horsemen. They were lodged in some low shepherd's tents near the wells.

May 28. - Early in the morning the Moors saddled their horses, and Ali's chief slave ordered me to get in readiness. In a little time the same messenger returned, and, taking my boy by the shoulder, told him in the Mandingo language, that "Ali was to be his master in future;" and then turning to me, "The business is settled at last," said he; "the boy, and everything but your horse, goes back to Bubaker, but you may take the old fool" (meaning Johnson the interpreter) "with you to Jarra." I made him no answer; but being shocked beyond description at the idea of losing the poor boy, I hastened to Ali, who was at breakfast before his tent, surrounded by many of his courtiers. I told him (perhaps in rather too passionate a strain), that whatever imprudence I had been guilty of in coming into his country, I thought I had already been sufficiently punished for it by being so long detained, and then plundered of all my little property; which, however, gave me no uneasiness when compared with what he had just now done to me. I observed that the boy whom he had now seized upon was not a slave, and had been accused of no offence; he was, indeed, one of my attendants, and his faithful services in that station had procured him his freedom. His fidelity and attachment had made him fellow me into my present situation, and, as he looked up to me for protection I could not see him deprived of his liberty without remonstrating against such an act as the height of cruelty and injustice. Ali made no reply, but, with a haughty air and malignant smile, told his interpreter that if I did not mount my horse immediately he would send me back likewise. There is something in the frown of a tyrant which rouses the most secret emotions of the heart: I could not suppress my feelings, and for once entertained an indignant wish to rid the world of such a monster.

Poor Demba was not less affected than myself. He had formed a strong attachment towards me, and had a cheerfulness of disposition which often beguiled the tedious hours of captivity.He was likewise a proficient in the Bambarra tongue, and promised on that account to be of great utility to me in future.But it was in vain to expect anything favourable to humanity from people who are strangers to its dictates.So, having shaken hands with this unfortunate boy, and blended my tears with his, assuring him, however, that I would do my utmost to redeem him, I saw him led off by three of Ali's slaves towards the camp at Bubaker.

When the Moors had mounted their horses I was ordered to follow them, and, after a toilsome journey through the woods in a very sultry day, we arrived in the afternoon at a walled village called Doombani, where we remained two days, waiting for the arrival of some horsemen from the northward.

On the 1st of June we departed from Doombani towards Jarra.Our company now amounted to two hundred men, all on horseback, for the Moors never use infantry in their wars.They appeared capable of enduring great fatigue; but from their total want of discipline our journey to Jarra was more like a fox-chase than the march of an army.

At Jarra I took up my lodging at the house of my old acquaintance, Daman Jumma, and informed him of everything that had befallen me.I particularly requested him to use his interest with Ali to redeem my boy, and promised him a bill upon Dr. Laidley for the value of two slaves the moment he brought him to Jarra.Daman very readily undertook to negotiate the business, but found that Ali considered the boy as my principal interpreter, and was unwilling to part with him, lest he should fall a second time into my hands, and be instrumental in conducting me to Bambarra.Ali, therefore, put off the matter from day to day, but withal told Daman that if he wished to purchase the boy for himself he should have him thereafter at the common price of a slave, which Daman agreed to pay for him whenever Ali should send him to Jarra.

The chief object of Ali, in this journey to Jarra, as I have already related, was to procure money from such of the Kaartans as had taken refuge in his country.Some of these had solicited his protection to avoid the horrors of war, but by far the greatest number of them were dissatisfied men, who wished the ruin of their own sovereign.These people no sooner heard that the Bambarra army had returned to Sego without subduing Daisy, as was generally expected, than they resolved to make a sudden attack themselves upon him before he could recruit his forces, which were now known to be much diminished by a bloody campaign, and in great want of provisions.With this view they solicited the Moors to join them, and offered to hire of Ali two hundred horsemen, which Ali, with the warmest professions of friendship, agreed to furnish, upon condition that they should previously supply him with four hundred head of cattle, two hundred garments of blue cloth, and a considerable quantity of beads and ornaments.

June 8. - In the afternoon Ali sent his chief slave to inform me that he was about to return to Bubaker: but as he would only stay there a few days to keep the approaching festival (Banna selee), and then return to Jarra, I had permission to remain with Daman until his return. This was joyful news to me; but I had experienced so many disappointments that I was unwilling to indulge the hope of its being true, until Johnson came and told me that Ali, with part of the horsemen, were actually gone from the town, and that the rest were to follow him in the morning.

June 9. - Early in the morning the remainder of the Moors departed from the town. They had, during their stay, committed many acts of robbery; and this morning with the most unparalleled audacity, they seized upon three girls who were bringing water from the wells, and carried them away into slavery.

June 12. - Two people, dreadfully wounded, were discovered at a watering-place in the woods; one of them had just breathed his last, but the other was brought alive to Jarra. On recovering a little he informed the people that he had fled through the woods from Kasson; that Daisy had made war upon Sambo, the king of that country; had surprised three of his towns, and put all the inhabitants to the sword. He enumerated by name many of the friends of the Jarra people who had been murdered in Kasson. This intelligence made the death-howl universal in Jarra for the space of two days.

This piece of bad news was followed by another not less distressing. A number of runaway slaves arrived from Kaarta on the 14th, and reported that Daisy, having received information concerning the intended attack upon him, was about to visit Jarra. This made the negroes call upon Ali for the two hundred horsemen which he was to furnish them according to engagement. But Ali paid very little attention to their remonstrances, and at last plainly told them that his cavalry were otherwise employed. The negroes, thus deserted by the Moors, and fully apprised that the king of Kaarta would show them as little clemency as he had shown the inhabitants of Kasson, resolved to collect all their forces, and hazard a battle before the king, who was now in great distress for want of provisions, should become too powerful for them. They therefore assembled about eight hundred effective men in the whole, and with these they entered Kaarta on the evening of the 18th of June.

June 19. - This morning the wind shifted to the south-west; and about two o'clock in the afternoon we had a heavy tornado, or thunder-squall, accompanied with rain, which greatly revived the face of nature, and gave a pleasant coolness to the air. This was the first rain that had fallen for many months.

As every attempt to redeem my boy had hitherto been unsuccessful, and in all probability would continue to prove so whilst I remained in the country, I found that it was necessary for me to come to some determination concerning my own safety before the rains should be fully set in; for my landlord, seeing no likelihood of being paid for his trouble, began to wish me away - and Johnson, my interpreter, refusing to proceed, my situation became very perplexing. I determined to avail myself of the first opportunity of escaping, and to proceed directly for Bambarra, as soon as the rains had set in for a few days, so as to afford me the certainty of finding water in the woods.

Such was my situation when, on the evening of the 24th of June, I was startled by the report of some muskets close to the town, and inquiring the reason, was informed that the Jarra army had returned from fighting Daisy, and that this firing was by way of rejoicing. However, when the chief men of the town had assembled, and heard a full detail of the expedition, they were by no means relieved from their uneasiness on Daisy's account. The deceitful Moors having drawn back from the confederacy, after being hired by the negroes, greatly dispirited the insurgents, who, instead of finding Daisy with a few friends concealed in the strong fortress of Gedingooma, had found him at a town near Joka, in the open country, surrounded by so numerous an army that every attempt to attack him was at once given up; and the confederates only thought of enriching themselves by the plunder of the small towns in the neighbourhood. They accordingly fell upon one of Daisy's towns, and carried off the whole of the inhabitants; but lest intelligence of this might reach Daisy, and induce him to cut off their retreat, they returned through the woods by night bringing with them the slaves and cattle which they had captured.

June 26. - This afternoon a spy from Kaarta brought the alarming intelligence that Daisy had taken Simbing in the morning, and would be in Jarra some time in the course of the ensuing day. Early in the morning nearly one-half of the townspeople took the road for Bambarra, by the way of Deena.

Their departure was very affecting, the women and children crying, the men sullen and dejected, and all of them looking back with regret on their native town, and on the wells and rocks beyond which their ambition had never tempted them to stray, and where they had laid all their plans of future happiness, all of which they were now forced to abandon, and to seek shelter among strangers.

June 27. - About eleven o'clock in the forenoon we were alarmed by the sentinels, who brought information that Daisy was on his march towards Jarra, and that the confederate army had fled before him without firing a gun. The terror of the townspeople on this occasion is not easily to be described. Indeed, the screams of the women and children, and the great hurry and confusion that everywhere prevailed, made me suspect that the

Kaartans had already entered the town; and although I had every reason to be pleased with Daisy's behaviour to me when I was at Kemmoo, I had no wish to expose myself to the mercy of his army, who might in the general confusion mistake me for a Moor. I therefore mounted my horse, and taking a large bag of corn before me, rode slowly along with the townspeople, until we reached the foot of a rocky hill, where I dismounted and drove my horse up before me. When I had reached the summit I sat down, and having a full view of the town and the neighbouring country, could not help lamenting the situation of the poor inhabitants, who were thronging after me, driving their sheep, cows, goats, andc., and carrying a scanty portion of provisions and a few clothes. There was a great noise and crying everywhere upon the road, for many aged people and children were unable to walk, and these, with the sick, were obliged to be carried, otherwise they must have been left to certain destruction.

About five o'clock we arrived at a small farm belonging to the Jarra people, called Kadeeja; and here I found Daman and Johnson employed in filling large bags of corn, to be carried upon bullocks, to serve as provisions for Daman's family on the road.

June 28. - At daybreak we departed from Kadeeja, and having passed Troongoomba without stopping, arrived in the afternoon at Queira. I remained here two days, in order to recruit my horse, which the Moors had reduced to a perfect Rosinante, and to wait for the arrival of some Mandingo negroes, who were going for Bambarra in the course of a few days.

On the afternoon of the 1st of July, as I was tending my horse in the fields, Ali's chief slave and four Moors arrived at Queira, and took up their lodging at the dooty's house. My interpreter, Johnson, who suspected the nature of this visit, sent two boys to overhear their conversation, from which he learnt that they were sent to convey me back to Bubaker. The same evening two of the Moors came privately to look at my horse, and one of them proposed taking it to the dooty's hut, but the other observed that such a precaution was unnecessary, as I could never escape upon such an animal. They then inquired where I slept, and returned to their companions,

All this was like a stroke of thunder to me, for I dreaded nothing so much as confinement again among the Moors, from whose barbarity I had nothing but death to expect. I therefore determined to set off immediately for Bambarra, a measure which I thought offered almost the only chance of saving my life and gaining the object of my mission. I communicated the design to Johnson, who, although he applauded my resolution, was so far from showing any inclination to accompany me, that he solemnly protested he would rather forfeit his wages than go any farther. He told me that Daman had agreed to give him half the price of a slave for his service to assist in conducting a coffle of slaves to Gambia, and that he was

determined to embrace the opportunity of returning to his wife and family.
Having no hopes, therefore, of persuading him to accompany me, I resolved to proceed by myself.About midnight I got my clothes in readiness, which consisted of two shirts, two pairs of trousers, two pocket-handkerchiefs, an upper and under waistcoat, a mat, and a pair of half-boots; these, with a cloak, constituted my whole wardrobe.And I had not one single bead, nor any other article of value in my possession, to purchase victuals for myself or corn for my horse.
About daybreak, Johnson, who had been listening to the Moors all night, came and whispered to me that they were asleep.The awful crisis was now arrived when I was again either to taste the blessing of freedom or languish out my days in captivity.A cold sweat moistened my forehead as I thought on the dreadful alternative, and reflected that, one way or another, my fate must be decided in the course of the ensuing day.But to deliberate was to lose the only chance of escaping.So, taking up my bundle, I stepped gently over the negroes, who were sleeping in the open air, and having mounted my horse, I bade Johnson farewell, desiring him to take particular care of the papers I had entrusted him with, and inform my friends in Gambia that he had left me in good health, on my way to Bambarra.
I proceeded with great caution, surveying each bush, and frequently listening and looking behind me for the Moorish horsemen, until I was about a mile from the town, when I was surprised to find myself in the neighbourhood of a korree belonging to the Moors.The shepherds followed me for about a mile, hooting and throwing stones after me; and when I was out of their reach, and had begun to indulge the pleasing hopes of escaping, I was again greatly alarmed to hear somebody holloa behind me, and looking back, I saw three Moors on horseback, coming after me at full speed, whooping and brandishing their double-barrelled guns.I knew it was in vain to think of escaping, and therefore turned back and met them, when two of them caught hold of my bridle, one on each side, and the third, presenting his musket, told me I must go back to Ali.When the human mind has for some time been fluctuating between hope and despair, tortured with anxiety, and hurried from one extreme to another, it affords a sort of gloomy relief to know the worst that can possibly happen.Such was my situation.An indifference about life and all its enjoyments had completely benumbed my faculties, and I rode back with the Moors with apparent unconcern.But a change took place much sooner than I had any reason to expect.In passing through some thick bushes one of the Moors ordered me to untie my bundle and show them the contents.Having examined the different articles, they found nothing worth taking except my cloak, which they considered as a very valuable acquisition, and one of them pulling it from me, wrapped it about himself, and, with one of his companions, rode off with their prize.When I attempted to follow them,

the third, who had remained with me, struck my horse over the head, and presenting his musket, told me I should proceed no farther. I now perceived that these men had not been sent by any authority to apprehend me, but had pursued me solely with a view to rob and plunder me. Turning my horse's head, therefore, once more towards the east, and observing the Moor follow the track of his confederates, I congratulated myself on having escaped with my life, though in great distress, from such a horde of barbarians.

I was no sooner out of sight of the Moor than I struck into the woods to prevent being pursued, and kept pushing on with all possible speed, until I found myself near some high rocks, which I remembered to have seen in my former route from Queira to Deena and, directing my course a little to the northward, I fortunately fell in with the path.

CHAPTER XIV

It is impossible to describe the joy that arose in my mind when I looked around and concluded that I was out of danger. I felt like one recovered from sickness; I breathed freer; I found unusual lightness in my limbs; even the desert looked pleasant; and I dreaded nothing so much as falling in with some wandering parties of Moors, who might convey me back to the land of thieves and murderers from which I had just escaped.

I soon became sensible, however, that my situation was very deplorable, for I had no means of procuring food nor prospect of finding water. About ten o'clock, perceiving a herd of goats feeding close to the road, I took a circuitous route to avoid being seen, and continued travelling through the wilderness, directing my course by compass nearly east-south-east, in order to reach as soon as possible some town or village of the kingdom of Bambarra.

A little after noon, when the burning heat of the sun was reflected with double violence from the hot sand, and the distant ridges of the hills, seen through the ascending vapour, seemed to wave and fluctuate like the unsettled sea, I became faint with thirst, and climbed a tree in hopes of seeing distant smoke, or some other appearance of a human habitation - but in vain: nothing appeared all around but thick underwood and hillocks of white sand.

About four o'clock I came suddenly upon a large herd of goats, and pulling my horse into a bush, I watched to observe if the keepers were Moors or negroes. In a little time I perceived two Moorish boys, and with some difficulty persuaded them to approach me. They informed me that the herd belonged to Ali, and that they were going to Deena, where the water was more plentiful, and where they intended to stay until the rain had filled the pools in the desert. They showed me their empty water-skins, and told me that they had seen no water in the woods. This account afforded me but little consolation; however, it was in vain to repine, and I pushed on as fast as possible, in hopes of reaching some watering-place in the course of the night. My thirst was by this time become insufferable; my mouth was parched and inflamed; a sudden dimness would frequently come over my eyes, with other symptoms of fainting; and my horse being very much fatigued, I began seriously to apprehend that I should perish of thirst. To relieve the burning pain in my mouth and throat I chewed the leaves of different shrubs, but found them all bitter, and of no service to me.

A little before sunset, having reached the top of a gentle rising, I climbed a high tree, from the topmost branches of which I cast a melancholy look over the barren wilderness, but without discovering the most distant trace of a human dwelling. The same dismal uniformity of shrubs and sand everywhere presented itself, and the horizon was as level and uninterrupted as that of the sea.

Descending from the tree, I found my horse devouring the stubble and brushwood with great avidity; and as I was now too faint to attempt walking, and my horse too much fatigued to carry me I thought it but an act of humanity, and perhaps the last I should ever have it in my power to perform, to take off his bridle and let him shift for himself, in doing which I was suddenly affected with sickness and giddiness, and falling upon the sand, felt as if the hour of death was fast approaching. Here, then, thought I, after a short but ineffectual struggle, terminate all my hopes of being useful in my day and generation; here must the short span of my life come to an end. I cast, as I believed, a last look on the surrounding scene, and whilst I reflected on the awful change that was about to take place, this world with its enjoyment seemed to vanish from my recollection. Nature, however, at length resumed its functions, and on recovering my senses, I found myself stretched upon the sand, with the bridle still in my hand, and the sun just sinking behind the trees. I now summoned all my resolution, and determined to make another effort to prolong my existence; and as the evening was somewhat cool, I resolved to travel as far as my limbs would carry me, in hopes of reaching - my only resource - a watering-place. With this view I put the bridle on my horse, and driving him before me, went slowly along for about an hour, when I perceived some lightning from the north-east - a most delightful sight, for it promised rain. The darkness and lightning increased very rapidly, and in less than an hour I heard the wind roaring among the bushes. I had already opened my mouth to receive the refreshing drops which I expected, but I was instantly covered with a cloud of sand, driven with such force by the wind as to give a very disagreeable sensation to my face and arms, and I was obliged to mount my horse and stop under a bush to prevent being suffocated. The sand continued to fly in amazing quantities for nearly an hour, after which I again set forward, and travelled with difficulty until ten o'clock. About this time I was agreeably surprised by some very vivid flashes of lightning, followed by a few heavy drops of rain. In a little time the sand ceased to fly, and I alighted and spread out all my clean clothes to collect the rain, which at length I saw would certainly fall. For more than an hour it rained plentifully, and I quenched my thirst by wringing and sucking my clothes.

There being no moon, it was remarkably dark, so that I was obliged to lead my horse, and direct my way by the compass, which the lightning enabled me to observe. In this manner I travelled with tolerable expedition until past midnight, when the lightning becoming more distant, I was under the necessity of groping along, to the no small danger of my hands and eyes. About two o'clock my horse started at something, and looking round, I was not a little surprised to see a light at a short distance among the trees; and supposing it to be a town, I groped along the sand in hopes of finding corn-stalks, cotton, or other appearances of cultivation, but found none. As I approached I perceived a number of other lights in different places, and began to suspect that I had fallen upon a party of Moors. However, in my present situation, I was resolved to see who they were, if I could do it with safety. I accordingly led my horse cautiously towards the light, and heard by the lowing of the cattle and the clamorous tongues of the herdsmen, that it was a watering-place, and most likely belonged to the Moors. Delightful as the sound of the human voice was to me, I resolved once more to strike into the woods, and rather run the risk of perishing of hunger than trust myself again in their hands; but being still thirsty, and dreading the approach of the burning day, I thought it prudent to search for the wells, which I expected to find at no great distance.

In this purpose I inadvertently approached so near to one of the tents as to be perceived by a woman, who immediately screamed out. Two people came running to her assistance from some of the neighbouring tents, and passed so very near to me that I thought I was discovered, and hastened again into the woods.

About a mile from this place I heard a loud and confused noise somewhere to the right of my course, and in a short time was happy to find it was the croaking of frogs, which was heavenly music to my ears. I followed the sound, and at daybreak arrived at some shallow muddy pools, so full of frogs, that it was difficult to discern the water. The noise they made frightened my horse, and I was obliged to keep them quiet, by beating the water with a branch, until he had drunk. Having here quenched my thirst, I ascended a tree, and the morning being calm, I soon perceived the smoke of the watering-place which I had passed in the night, and observed another pillar of smoke east-south-east, distant twelve or fourteen miles. Towards this I directed my route, and reached the cultivated ground a little before eleven o'clock, where, seeing a number of negroes at work planting corn, I inquired the name of the town, and was informed that it was a Foulah village belonging to Ali, called Shrilla. I had now some doubts about entering it; but my horse being very much fatigued, and the day growing hot - not to mention the pangs of hunger, which began to assail me - I resolved to venture; and accordingly rode up to the dooty's house, where I was unfortunately denied admittance, and could not obtain oven a handful of corn either for myself or horse. Turning from this inhospitable door, I rode slowly out of the town, and, perceiving some low, scattered huts without the walls, I directed my route towards them, knowing that in Africa, as well as in Europe, hospitality does not always prefer the highest dwellings. At the door of one of these huts an old motherly-looking woman sat, spinning cotton. I made signs to her that I was hungry, and inquired if she had any victuals with her in the hut. She immediately laid down her distaff, and desired me, in Arabic, to come in. When I had seated myself upon the floor, she set before me a dish of kouskous that had been left the preceding night, of which I made a tolerable meal; and in return for this kindness I gave her one of my pocket-handkerchiefs, begging at the same time a little corn for my horse, which she readily brought me.

Whilst my horse was feeding the people began to assemble, and one of them whispered something to my hostess which very much excited her surprise. Though I was not well acquainted with the Foulah language, I soon discovered that some of the men wished to apprehend and carry me back to Ali, in hopes, I suppose, of receiving a reward. I therefore tied up the corn; and lest any one should suspect I had run away from the Moors, I took a northerly direction, and went cheerfully along, driving my horse before me, followed by all the boys and girls of the town. When I had travelled about two miles, and got quit of all my troublesome attendants, I struck again into the woods, and took shelter under a large tree, where I found it necessary to rest myself, a bundle of twigs serving me for a bed, and my saddle for a pillow.

July 4. - At daybreak I pursued my course through the woods as formerly; saw numbers of antelopes, wild hogs, and ostriches, but the soil was more hilly, and not so fertile as I had found it the preceding day. About eleven o'clock I ascended an eminence, where I climbed a tree, and discovered, at about eight miles' distance, an open part of the country, with several red spots, which I concluded were cultivated land, and, directing my course that way, came to the precincts of a watering-place about one o'clock. From the appearance of the place, I judged it to belong to the Foulahs, and was hopeful that I should meet a better reception than I had experienced at Shrilla. In this I was not deceived, for one of the shepherds invited me to come into his tent and partake of some dates. This was one of those low Foulah tents in which there is room just sufficient to sit upright, and in which the family, the furniture, andc., seem huddled together like so many articles in a chest. When I had crept upon my hands and knees into this humble habitation, I found that it contained a woman and three children, who, together with the shepherd and myself, completely occupied the floor. A dish of boiled corn and dates was produced, and the master of the family, as is customary in this part of the country, first tasted it himself, and then desired me to follow his example. Whilst I was eating, the children kept their eyes fixed upon me, and no sooner did the shepherd pronounce the word Nazarani, than they began to cry, and their mother crept slowly towards the door, out of which she sprang like a greyhound, and was instantly followed by her children. So frightened were they at the very name of a Christian, that no entreaties could induce them to approach the tent. Here I purchased some corn for my horse, in exchange for some brass buttons, and having thanked the shepherd for his hospitality, struck again into the woods. At sunset I came to a road that took the direction for Bambarra, and resolved to follow it for the night; but about eight o'clock, hearing some people coming from the southward, I thought it prudent to hide myself among some thick bushes near the road. As these thickets are generally full of wild beasts, I found my situation rather unpleasant, sitting in the dark, holding my horse by the nose with both hands, to prevent him from neighing, and equally afraid of the natives without and the wild beasts within. My fears, however, were soon dissipated; for the people, after looking round the thicket, and perceiving nothing, went away, and I hastened to the more open parts of the wood, where I pursued my journey east-south-east, until past midnight, when the joyful cry of frogs induced me once more to deviate a little from my route, in order to quench my thirst. Having accomplished this from a large pool of rain-water, I sought for an open place, with a single tree in the midst, under which I made my bed for the night. I was disturbed by some wolves towards morning, which induced me to set forward a little before day; and having passed a small village called Wassalita, I came about ten o'clock (July 5th), to a negro town called Wawra, which properly belongs to Kaarta, but was at this time tributary to Mansong, King of Bambarra.

CHAPTER XV

Wawra is a small town surrounded with high walls, and inhabited by a mixture of Mandingoes and Foulahs. The inhabitants employ themselves chiefly in cultivating corn, which they exchange with the Moors for salt. Here, being in security from the Moors, and very much fatigued, I resolved to rest myself; and meeting with a hearty welcome from the dooty, whose name was Flancharee, I laid myself down upon a bullock's hide, and slept soundly for about two hours. The curiosity of the people would not allow me to sleep any longer. They had seen my saddle and bridle, and were assembled in great numbers to learn who I was and whence I came. Some were of opinion that I was an Arab; others insisted that I was some Moorish Sultan, and they continued to debate the matter with such warmth that the noise awoke me. The dooty (who had formerly been at Gambia) at last interposed in my behalf, and assured them that I was certainly a white man; but he was convinced from my appearance that I was a poor one.

July 6. - It rained very much in the night, and at daylight I departed in company with a negro who was going to a town called Dingyee for corn; but we had not proceeded above a mile before the ass upon which he rode threw him off, and he returned, leaving me to prosecute the journey by myself.

I reached Dingyee about noon, but the dooty and most of the inhabitants had gone into the fields to cultivate corn. An old Foulah, observing me wandering about the town, desired me to come to his hut, where I was well entertained; and the dooty, when he returned, sent me some victuals for myself and corn for my horse.

July 7. - In the morning, when I was about to depart, my landlord, with a great deal of diffidence, begged me to give him a lock of my hair. He had been told, he said, that white men's hair made a saphie that would give to the possessor all the knowledge of white men. I had never before heard of so simple a mode of education, but instantly complied with the request.

I reached a small town called Wassiboo, about twelve o'clock, where I was obliged to stop until an opportunity should offer of procuring a guide to Satilé, which is distant a very long day's journey, through woods without any beaten path. I accordingly took up my residence at the dooty's house, where I stayed four days, during which time I amused myself by going to the fields with the family to plant corn. Cultivation is carried on here on a very extensive scale; and, as the natives themselves express it, "Hunger is never known." In cultivating the soil the men and women work together. They use a large sharp hoe, much superior to that used in Gambia, but they are obliged, for fear of the Moors, to carry their arms with them to the field. The master, with the handle of his spear, marks the field into regular plats, one of which is assigned to every three slaves.

On the evening of the 11th eight of the fugitive Kaartans arrived at Wassiboo. They had found it impossible to live under the tyrannical government of the Moors, and were now going to transfer their allegiance to the King of Bambarra. They offered to take me along with them as far as Satilé, and I accepted the offer.

July 12. - At daybreak we set out, and travelled with uncommon expedition until sunset. We stopped only twice in the course of the day, once at a watering-place in the woods, and at another time at the ruins of a town formerly belonging to Daisy, called Illa-compe (the corn-town). When we arrived in the neighbourhood of Satilé, the people who were employed in the corn-fields, seeing so many horsemen, took us for a party of Moors, and ran screaming away from us. The whole town was instantly alarmed, and the slaves were seen in every direction driving the cattle and horses towards the town. It was in vain that one of our company galloped up to undeceive them; it only frightened them the more; and when we arrived at the town we found the gates shut, and the people all under arms. After a long parley we were permitted to enter, and, as there was every appearance of a tornado, the dooty allowed us to sleep in his baloon, and gave us each a bullock's hide for a bed.

July 13. - Early in the morning we again set forward. The roads were wet and slippery, but the country was very beautiful, abounding with rivulets, which were increased by the rain into rapid streams. About ten o'clock we came to the rains of a village which had been destroyed by war about six months before.

About noon my horse was so much fatigued that I could not keep up with my companions; I therefore dismounted, and desired them to ride on, telling them that I would follow as soon as my horse had rested a little. But I found them unwilling to leave me; the lions, they said, were very numerous in those parts, and though they might not so readily attack a body of people, they would soon find out an individual; it was therefore agreed that one of the company should stay with me to assist in driving my horse, while the others passed on to Galloo to procure lodgings, and collect grass for the horses before night. Accompanied by this worthy negro, I drove my horse before me until about four o'clock, when we came in sight of Galloo, a considerable town, standing in a fertile and beautiful valley surrounded with high rocks.

Early next morning (July 14th), having first returned many thanks to our landlord for his hospitality, while my fellow-travellers offered up their prayers that he might never want, we set forward, and about three o'clock arrived at Moorja, a large town, famous for its trade in salt, which the Moors bring here in great quantities, to exchange for corn and cotton cloth. As most of the people here are Mohammedans, it is not allowed to the kafirs to drink beer, which they call neodollo (corn spirit), except in certain houses. In one of these I saw about twenty people sitting round large vessels of this beer with the greatest conviviality, many of them in a state of intoxication.

On the morning of the 16th we again set forward, accompanied by a coffle of fourteen asses, loaded with salt, bound for Sansanding. The road was particularly romantic, between two rocky hills; but the Moors sometimes lie in wait here to plunder strangers. As soon as we had reached the open country the master of the salt coffle thanked us for having stayed with him so long, and now desired us to ride on. The sun was almost set before we reached Datliboo. In the evening we had a most tremendous tornado. The house in which we lodged being flat-roofed, admitted the rain in streams; the floor was soon ankle-deep, the fire extinguished, and we were left to pass the night upon some bundles of firewood that happened to lie in a corner.

July 17. - We departed from Datliboo, and about ten o'clock passed a large coffle returning from Sego with corn-hoes, mats, and other household utensils. At five o'clock we came to a large village where we intended to pass the night, but the dooty would not receive us. When we departed from this place my horse was so much fatigued that I was under the necessity of driving him, and it was dark before we reached Fanimboo, a small village, the dooty of which no sooner heard that I was a white man than he brought out three old muskets, and was much disappointed when he was told that I could not repair them.

July 18. - We continued our journey, but, owing to a light supper the preceding night we felt ourselves rather hungry this morning, and endeavoured to procure some corn at a village, but without success.

My horse becoming weaker and weaker every day, was now of very little service to me; I was obliged to drive him before me for the greater part of the day, and did not reach Geosorro until eight o'clock in the evening. I found my companions wrangling with the dooty, who had absolutely refused to give or sell them any provisions; and as none of us had tasted victuals for the last twenty-four hours, we were by no means disposed to fast another day if we could help it. But finding our entreaties without effect, and being very much fatigued, I fell asleep, from which I was awakened about midnight with the joyful information Kinne nata! ("The victuals are come")This made the remainder of the night pass away pleasantly, and at daybreak, July 19th, we resumed our journey, proposing to stop at a village called Doolinkeaboo for the night following. My fellow-travellers, having better horses than myself, soon left me, and I was walking barefoot, driving my horse, when I was met by a coffle of slaves, about seventy in number, coming from Sego. They were tied together by their necks with thongs of a bullock's hide, twisted like a rope - seven slaves upon a thong, and a man with a musket between every seven. Many of the slaves were ill-conditioned, and a great number of them women. In the rear came Sidi Mahomed's servant, whom I remembered to have seen at the camp of Benowm. He presently knew me, and told me that these slaves were going to Morocco by the way of Ludamar and the Great Desert.

In the afternoon, as I approached Doolinkeaboo, I met about twenty Moors on horseback, the owners of the slaves I had seen in the morning. They were well armed with muskets, and were very inquisitive concerning me, but not so rude as their countrymen generally are. From them I learned that Sidi Mahomed was not at Sego, but had gone to Kancaba for gold-dust.

When I arrived at Doolinkeaboo I was informed that my fellow-travellers had gone on, but my horse was so much fatigued that I could not possibly proceed after them. The dooty of the town at my request gave me a draught of water, which is generally looked upon as an earnest of greater hospitality, and I had no doubt of making up for the toils of the day by a good supper and a sound sleep; unfortunately, I had neither the one nor the other. The night was rainy and tempestuous, and the dooty limited his hospitality to the draught of water.

July 20. - In the morning I endeavoured, both by entreaties and threats, to procure some victuals from the dooty, but in vain. I even begged some corn from one of his female slaves, as she was washing it at the well, and had the mortification to be refused. However, when the dooty was gone to the fields, his wife sent me a handful of meal, which I mixed with water and drank for breakfast. About eight o'clock I departed from Doolinkeaboo, and at noon stopped a few minutes at a large korree, where I had some milk given me by the Foulahs, and hearing that two negroes were going from thence to Sega, I was happy to have their company, and we set out immediately. About four o'clock we stopped at a small village, where one of the negroes met with an acquaintance, who invited us to a sort of public entertainment, which was conducted with more than common propriety. A dish, made of sour milk and meal, called sinkatoo, and beer made from their corn, was distributed with great liberality, and the women were admitted into the society, a circumstance I had never before observed in Africa. There was no compulsion - every one was at liberty to drink as he pleased - they nodded to each other when about to drink, and on setting down the calabash commonly said Berka ("Thank you"). Both men and women appeared to be somewhat intoxicated, but they were far from being quarrelsome.

Departing from thence, we passed several large villages, where I was constantly taken for a Moor and became the subject of much merriment to the Bambarrans, who, seeing me drive my horse before me, laughed heartily at my appearance. "He has been at Mecca," says one, "you may see that by his clothes;" another asked me if my horse was sick; a third wished to purchase it, andc., so that, I believe, the very slaves were ashamed to be seen in my company. Just before it was dark we took up our lodging for the night at a small village, where I procured some victuals for myself and some corn for my horse, at the moderate price of a button; and was told that I should see the Niger (which the negroes call Joliba, or the Great Water) early the next day. The lions are here very numerous; the gates are shut a little after sunset, and nobody allowed to go out. The thoughts of seeing the Niger in the morning, and the troublesome buzzing of mosquitoes, prevented me from shutting my eyes during the night; and I had saddled my horse, and was in readiness before daylight, but, on account of the wild beasts, we were obliged to wait until the people were stirring and the gates opened. This happened to be a market day at Sego, and the roads were everywhere filled with people carrying different articles to sell. We passed four large villages, and at eight o'clock saw the smoke over Sego.

As we approached the town I was fortunate enough to overtake the fugitive Kaartans, to whose kindness I had been so much indebted in my journey through Bambarra. They readily agreed to introduce me to the king; and we rode together through some marshy ground, where, as I was anxiously looking around for the river, one of them called out, Geo affili! ("See the water!") and, looking forwards, I saw with infinite pleasure the great object of my mission - the long-sought-for majestic Niger, glittering in the morning sun, as broad as the Thames at Westminster, and flowing slowly to the eastward. I hastened to the brink, and having drunk of the water, lifted up my fervent thanks in prayer to the Great Ruler of all things for having thus far crowned my endeavours with success.

The circumstance of the Niger's flowing towards the east, and its collateral points, did not, however, excite my surprise, for, although I had left Europe in great hesitation on this subject, and rather believed that it ran in the contrary direction, I had made such frequent inquiries during my progress concerning this river, and received from the negroes of different nations such clear and decisive assurances that its general course was towards the rising sun, as scarce left any doubt on my mind, and more especially as I knew that Major Houghton had collected similar information in the same manner.

Sego, the capital of Bambarra, at which I had now arrived, consists, properly speaking, of four distinct towns - two on the northern bank of the Niger, called Sego Korro and Sego Boo; and two on the southern bank, called Sego Soo Korro and Sego See Korro. They are all surrounded with high mud walls. The houses are built of clay, of a square form with flat roofs - some of them have two storeys, and many of them are whitewashed. Besides these buildings, Moorish mosques are seen in every quarter; and the streets, though narrow, are broad enough for every useful purpose, in a country where wheel carriages are entirely unknown. From the best inquiries I could make, I have reason to believe that Sego contains altogether about thirty thousand inhabitants. The King of Bambarra constantly resides at Sego See Korro. He employs a great many slaves in conveying people over the river, and the money they receive (though the fare is only ten kowrie shells for each individual) furnishes a considerable revenue to the king in the course of a year. The canoes are of a singular construction, each of them being formed of the trunks of two large trees rendered concave, and joined together, not side by side, but endways - the junction being exactly across the middle of the canoe: they are therefore very long, and disproportionably narrow, and have neither decks nor masts:

they are, however, very roomy, for I observed in one of them four horses and several people crossing over the river. When we arrived at this ferry, with a view to pass over to that part of the town in which the king resides, we found a great number waiting for a passage: they looked at me with silent wonder, and I distinguished with concern many Moors among them. There were three different places of embarkation, and the ferrymen were very diligent and expeditious; but from the crowd of people I could not immediately obtain a passage, and sat down upon the bank of the river to wait for a more favourable opportunity. The view of this extensive city - the numerous canoes upon the river - the crowded population, and the cultivated state of the surrounding country - formed altogether a prospect of civilisation and magnificence which I little expected to find in the bosom of Africa.

I waited more than two hours without having an opportunity of crossing the river, during which time the people who had crossed carried information to Mansong, the king, that a white man was waiting for a passage, and was coming to see him. He immediately sent over one of his chief men, who informed me that the king could not possibly see me until he knew what had brought me into his country; and that I must not presume to cross the river without the king's permission. He therefore advised me to lodge at a distant village, to which he pointed, for the night, and said that in the morning he would give me further instructions how to conduct myself. This was very discouraging. However, as there was no remedy, I set off for the village, where I found, to my great mortification, that no person would admit me into his house. I was regarded with astonishment and fear, and was obliged to sit all day without victuals in the shade of a tree; and the night threatened to be very uncomfortable - for the wind rose, and there was great appearance of a heavy rain - and the wild beasts are so very numerous in the neighbourhood that I should have been under the necessity of climbing up a tree and resting amongst the branches. About sunset, however, as I was preparing to pass the night in this manner, and had turned my horse loose that he might graze at liberty, a woman, returning from the labours of the field, stopped to observe me, and perceiving that I was weary and dejected, inquired into my situation, which I briefly explained to her; whereupon, with looks of great compassion, she took up my saddle and bridle, and told me to follow her. Having conducted me into her hut, she lighted up a lamp, spread a mat on the floor, and told me I might remain there for the night. Finding that I was very hungry, she said she would procure me something to eat. She accordingly went out, and returned in a short time with a very fine fish, which, having caused to be half broiled upon some embers, she gave me for supper. The rites of hospitality being thus performed towards a stranger in distress, my worthy benefactress (pointing to the mat, and telling me I might sleep there without apprehension) called to the female part of her family, who had stood gazing on me all the while in fixed astonishment, to resume their task of spinning cotton, in which they continued to employ themselves great part of the night. They lightened their labour by songs, one of which was composed extempore, for I was myself the subject of it. It was sung by one of the young women, the rest joining in a sort of chorus. The air was sweet and plaintive, and the words, literally translated, were these:- "The winds roared, and the rains fell. The poor white man, faint and weary, came and sat under our tree. He has no mother to bring him milk, no wife to grind his corn. Chorus. - Let us pity the white man, no mother has he," andc. andc. Trifling as this recital may appear to the reader, to a person in my situation the circumstance was affecting in the highest degree. I was oppressed by such unexpected kindness, and sleep fled from my eyes. In the morning I presented my compassionate landlady with two of the four brass buttons which remained on my waistcoat - the only recompense I could make her.

July 21. - I continued in the village all this day in conversation with the natives, who came in crowds to see me, but was rather uneasy towards evening to find that no message had arrived from the king, the more so as the people began to whisper that Mansong had received some very unfavourable accounts of me from the Moors and slatees residing at Sego, who, it seems, were exceedingly suspicious concerning the motives of my journey. I learned that many consultations had been held with the king concerning my reception and disposal; and some of the villagers frankly told me that I had many enemies, and must expect no favour.

July 22. - About eleven o'clock a messenger arrived from the king, but he gave me very little satisfaction. He inquired particularly if I had brought any present, and seemed much disappointed when he was told that I had been robbed of everything by the Moors. When I proposed to go along with him, he told me to stop until the afternoon, when the king would send for me.

July 23. - In the afternoon another messenger arrived from Mansong, with a bag in his hands. He told me it was the king's pleasure that I should depart forthwith from the vicinage of Sego; but that Mansong, wishing to relieve a white man in distress, had sent me five thousand kowries, to enable me to purchase provisions in the course of my journey: the messenger added, that if my intentions were really to proceed to Jenné, he had orders to accompany me as a guide to Sansanding. I was at first puzzled to account for this behaviour of the king; but from the conversation I had with the guide, I had afterwards reason to believe that Mansong would willingly have admitted me into his presence at Sego, but was apprehensive he might not be able to protect me against the blind and inveterate malice of the Moorish inhabitants. His conduct, therefore, was at once prudent and liberal. The circumstances under which I made my appearance at Sego were undoubtedly such as might create in the mind of the king a well-warranted suspicion that I wished to conceal the true object of my journey. He argued, probably, as my guide argued, who, when he was told that I had come from a great distance, and through many dangers, to behold the Joliba river, naturally inquired if there were no rivers in my own country, and whether one river was not like another. Notwithstanding this, and in spite of the jealous machinations of the Moors, this benevolent prince thought it sufficient that a white man was found in his dominions, in a condition of extreme wretchedness, and that no other plea was necessary to entitle the sufferer to his bounty.

FOOTNOTES

{1} I believe that similar charms or amulets, under the names of domini, grigri, fetich, andc., are common in all parts of Africa.

{2} Maana is within a short distance of the ruins of Fort St. Joseph, on the Senegal river, formerly a French factory.

Printed in Great Britain
by Amazon